With No Crying

By Celia Fremlin

WITH NO CRYING
THE SPIDER-ORCHID
THE LONG SHADOW
BY HORROR HAUNTED
APPOINTMENT WITH YESTERDAY
DON'T GO TO SLEEP IN THE DARK
POSSESSION
PRISONER'S BASE
THE JEALOUS ONE
SEVEN LEAN YEARS
UNCLE PAUL
THE HOURS BEFORE DAWN

With No Crying

CELIA FREMLIN

PUBLISHED FOR THE CRIME CLUB BY

DOUBLEDAY & COMPANY, INC.

GARDEN CITY, NEW YORK

1981

All of the characters in this book
are fictitious, and any resemblance
to actual persons, living or dead,
is purely coincidental.

ISBN: 0-385-17206-0
Library of Congress Catalog Card Number 80-1034

Printed in the United States of America

How can there be a cherry that has no stone?
How can there be a chicken that has no bone?
How can there be a thimble that has no rim?
How can there be a baby with no crying?

—"The Riddle Song," traditional

With No Crying

CHAPTER 1

She looked terribly young to be pregnant, but all the same she made a charming picture in her bright, flowered maternity smock, with her fair hair bouncing against her shoulders as she stepped along the sunny pavement. The women passing by, especially the older ones, whose child-bearing days were over, would give her a quick, furtive glance of curiosity not unmixed with envy; recalling, perhaps, the days when they, too, had dwelt at the throbbing heart of things, carrying within them the whole secret of life.

Eight months gone at the very least, they reckoned, slewing their eyes quickly away after a swift, knowledgeable glance at the billowing curve of gay cotton. More like nine, really—any minute, in fact—and yet how well she held herself still! Straight as a flower, her movements easy and graceful despite that hugely bulging belly: none of that ugly, waddling, side-to-side motion usually so characteristic of these last weeks of pregnancy. Remembering, perhaps, their own variegated discomforts and disabilities at this late stage—the varicose veins, the heartburn, the endless, lumbering tiredness—they envied her still more. Oh, well. Some girls have all the luck.

Miranda, looking neither to the left nor to the right, was nevertheless acutely aware of the sidelong, appraising glances; aware, too, of the covert envy and curiosity she was evoking. She could even, in a remote sort of way, enjoy it; for after all, these women were all of them total strangers to her, none of them was ever going to see her again. Not one of them would ever know that under the flamboyantly voluminous smock and the carefully contrived padding, there lay a stomach as flat as a boy's, and a hollow, empty womb.

Deceiving this crowd of casual, passing strangers was easy, even exhilarating. There were moments when she actually *felt* like a young mother, with a real live baby inside her, under the warmth of those anonymous, half-admiring stares.

It was deceiving her *friends* that was so awful—more and more intolerably awful with every passing day. Friends who had been so kind to her, so full of sympathy; who had taken her in so readily, and without question, passionately defending her right to unmarried motherhood, silencing any hint of criticism from outsiders, and resolutely refusing to let her take her turn at carrying down the garbage. By now, they were even buying advance toys for the baby, and beginning to knit things.

And all the time this thing that she nourished inside her, this thing whose arrival they all awaited with such generous enthusiasm, was not a real baby at all, but a monstrous bulge of lies and treachery, growing bigger and bigger day by day, just as a real baby would have done.

Numb with dread, and only dimly aware of the direction she was taking, Miranda continued on her apparently cool and unflurried way through the jostling crowds, the half-envious glances and fleeting smiles pattering like gentle rain upon the carapace of her guilt and fear. In the sweltering August heat, she was chilled through and through as though by some terminal illness.

On she went, slower and slower as her destination loomed nearer. With mounting horror, she visualised the warm and kindly welcome that awaited her, inexorably, when she reached the flat: the affectionate concern, the eager, solicitous questions.

"No, not yet," she would have to tell them, yet again: and then—she had taken to adding this of late, in desperation—"They think I must have got my dates wrong."

And someone would urge her to put her feet up. Another would bring her a nice cup of tea, sugared exactly right . . . and she would feel worse than any murderer, any traitor, because these were her *friends* whom she must betray, not her enemies, and for her there was no possibility of any last-minute reprieve. The dates couldn't go on being wrong forever; nor could the baby remain vaguely "overdue" much longer.

Catastrophe was upon her: humiliation beyond anything she could ever have imagined. And yet even now, even in this extremity of shame and terror, the idea of simply returning to Mummy and Daddy in their pleasant suburban house—with their pleasantly permissive principles and their vaguely left-wing broad-mindedness about vaguely everything—never for one moment crossed her mind.

CHAPTER 2

It was May when it had all begun, one of the loveliest Mays in living memory. For Miranda Field and her friend Sharon Whittaker, it looked like being the best summer term ever. Already enjoying many of the Upper School privileges—a coffee machine, for instance, and free periods for private study—they were nevertheless not yet properly in the grip of exams. O-levels were still a full year away and casting only the faintest of barely noticeable shadows across the golden months intervening. In this timeless unrepeatable interlude between childhood and the burdens of preparing for an adult career, it seemed downright ungrateful—almost a sin, really—to be working at all hard, and so Miranda and Sharon (clever girls anyway, to whom the school work came easily) nudged and whispered their way through the sunlit, easy-going lessons, and spent the long, delicious hours of "private study" lying in the long grass that bordered the playing fields, giggling, imagining, and egging one another on into being in love.

To an observer (if such there had been) looking down on them through the great white heads of cow parsley, and listening to the rapturous whispered confidences borne on the soft, sweet-scented airs of spring, it might have seemed that they were merely in love with love.

And perhaps they were. But what of it? There is nothing "mere" about this kind of love, especially if you are not quite fifteen and drunk with the returning sun. And in any case, they had each of them, according to her questing fancy, given to this abstract passion a temporary incarnation and a name from among the remote and inaccessible sixth-formers at the top of the school. Thus Sharon was madly, hopelessly in love with the school cricket captain, one Gordon Hargreaves, tall and fair, lithe as a whip, and as brilliant at work as he was at games; while Miranda, not to be outdone, had succeeded in working herself into a delicious state of unrequited passion for the secretary of the Sixth Form Chess Club, a dark, saturnine youth with shining almond-shaped eyes and black, springy hair lifting from his scalp as if blown by some eternal wind. His name was Trevor Marks, and he played the zither as well as chess; and sometimes Miranda, catcing the faint, distant twang of the instrument through the windows of the Sixth Form Common Room, would almost faint for joy standing out there on the gravel path in the sunshine, the books for whatever class she was on her way to clasped ecstatically against her pounding heart.

The joy of it was beyond belief; and while the magical springtime burgeoned towards summer, and branches heavy with may looped low above their giggling heads, they would whisper low to one another about the latest crop of wonders. How Gordon the cricket captain had been glimpsed putting his cycling clips on and mounting his bicycle yesterday afternoon just by the school gate; or how Trevor (Miranda's one) had almost collided with her as he raced down the steps of the Science Block, evidently late for something.

Suppose they had *actually* collided, Miranda rapturously surmised, her eyes half-closed against the incredible blueness of the sky: suppose he had knocked her right to the bottom, and had then kneeled by her, white-faced with concern, his hand on her breast to make sure her heart was still beating . . . And then again (for fair's fair, and Sharon was entitled to her turn) suppose that, mounting his bicycle, Gordon Hargreaves had caught sight of Sharon, her newly washed hair lapping almost to her waist, and had paused for a moment to wonder who she was, and why he'd never noticed her before? Leaning his bicycle carefully and deliberately against the fence, suppose he'd strolled towards her, with a look of growing wonder in his laughing blue eyes . . .

Supposing . . . supposing . . . ! It was no wonder that the actual experiences of the supposedly luckier girls who had real-life, flesh-and-blood boyfriends, seemed tame indeed in comparison, not to say depressing. Listening, on Monday mornings, to the variegated setbacks and traumas endured over the weekend by their ostensibly more fortunate classmates—the tales of telephone calls that never came; of dates that ended in tears and recriminations; of being kept waiting; of being stood-up; of being kissed "like that," and of *not* being kissed "like that"; of unloving words and of uncouth behaviour; of being taller than him and looking like a pair of Charlies walking along together—listening to all this, Miranda and Sharon could hardly help, sometimes, giving way to a deep, secret conviction of their own superior good fortune.

Because, of course, there was no way in which *their* loved ones could fail them in this sort of distressing fashion—or indeed in any fashion. Since neither Gordon the cricket captain nor Trevor the chess champion had ever spoken to either of the girls, or were even aware of their existence, there was absolutely no way in which they could let them down. No way in which they could slight them, neglect them, be unfaithful to them or even (God forbid!) bore them.

There is something in human nature which cannot leave well alone, which is somehow impelled to interfere, to provoke change, in no matter how blissful and ideal a situation. Thus it was with Miranda and Sharon, the precipitating factor in their case being the school dance, billed to take place at the end of May, on the last Friday before half-term.

Naturally enough, the occasion seemed, in prospect, to present unprecedented opportunities to anyone in the throes of undeclared and unrequited love. For the dance was one of the few occasions in the school year when the normal barriers of hierarchy, age, and status could be expected to break down, and it would actually become possible for a fourth-former to walk up to a top prefect and say—Well, say *something*, anyway . . .

What they would say, when and how they would summon up the courage to say it, required quite a bit of advance planning, and in the end they settled for a scheme both simple and ingenious: each girl, at some time during the evening, was to walk boldly up to the *other* one's beloved and offer to introduce him to "my friend." The idea seemed to both of them a brilliant one, and very nearly foolproof, for this way each girl only risked a snub from the boy she *wasn't* in love with, and so suicide would be unnecessary.

Simple enough in conception, the plan proved by no means so easy of execution. The difficulties surged in upon them in a blast of noise and heat and colour the moment they set foot in the big hall where the dance was being held. Somehow they hadn't quite envisaged all this crush . . . all this din. Even to *find* their unsuspecting prey would be a mammoth task; and as for waiting around for an appropriate moment—"*Not* while he's talking to someone," they'd promised each other beforehand, "*and* not if he looks busy . . . or preoccupied . . . or in a hurry"—such niceties would clearly have to go by the board. They'd be lucky if they even got a glimpse of their respective victims, either of them.

Still, they weren't the sort of girls to give up easily. Twice . . . thrice . . . they prowled the length and breadth of the dance hall, peering ferociously into the undergrowth of bright dresses and swaying bodies; and it was only when, after a few more turns, they decided to give themselves a breather out in the cool of the corridor, that suddenly it all happened. All at once the swing doors at the far end burst apart at the impact of a fresh band of revellers, and almost without warning Miranda found herself less than a yard from her friend's beloved as he hurried past with an ice cream cone in each hand.

There was no escape. It had happened: and only now did Miranda realise how deeply she'd been counting on the probability that it wouldn't. She felt her mouth go dry, and her knees shook, even though he *wasn't* the one she was in love with.

"Would you like to meet my friend, Sharon Whittaker?" she blurted out. He stopped at once, looking a bit surprised, but smiling down at her amiably enough.

"Sorry, love—" he gestured apologetically with the near-side ice cream, "Later on—d'you mind?" and with another vague gesture of distracted goodwill, he disappeared through the door into the crowded dance hall, and vanished from their sight.

Well, at least he hadn't snubbed her. He'd been nice enough, it hadn't been a disaster; but on the other hand you couldn't call it a success, either. Disappointing, especially for Sharon.

Still, he might come back. His words had vaguely implied something of the kind, had they not? For a while, the two conspirators hung about in the doorway, their eyes darting this way and that among the crowd, bright and intent as blackbirds watching for worms.

But he didn't come; and presently, when they began to realise it was hopeless, it became necessary to apply their minds to the next item on the agenda—Trevor Marks. It was Sharon who must stick her neck out this time, and see if she could do better on Miranda's behalf than Miranda had on hers.

Systematically she set about her task, working her way back and forth across the packed dance floor, quartering the ground, with Miranda like a gun dog close on her heels.

It didn't take so long this time. Within a very few minutes they had their quarry cornered, and proceeded, with a fine display of averted eyes and calculated unconcern, to close in on him. It so happened that at this particular moment Trevor Marks was deeply engaged in conversation—but what of it? The conversation was only with another boy, and therefore didn't count. Planting herself sturdily in the victim's direct line of vision, Sharon boldly interrupted in mid-sentence whatever it was he was saying.

"May I introduce my friend Mira—?" she was beginning—then took a step back in surprise as he immediately whirled round on her with a dazzling smile, beaming it first upon her and then swivelling it expertly towards Miranda.

"Hi!" he greeted them collectively. "Can I get you both a drink? Cider?—No, wait, I've a better idea. Stay here, don't go away, there's good girls, I'll be back in a sec—"

But by the time he returned, a glass of foaming beer in each hand, Sharon had loyally (and according to plan) disappeared.

"Where's your friend?" he asked, glancing round enquiringly; and Miranda, opening her mouth to reply, found herself incapable of uttering a single word. It was as if she'd suffered a stroke, like an old woman of ninety, right there on the dance floor.

Never mind about being witty and brilliant, as in her dreams; all she could pray for now was the strength to say *something*. Anything.

"I don't . . . that is . . . well, she was here a minute ago," she managed at last, and tried to hide her burning cheeks by raising her glass and taking a gulp of beer. It tasted awful.

"Oh." He didn't pursue the subject; and after a few more halting exchanges ("What class are you in, then?"

"Four A." "You like it there?" "It's O.K."), the conversation ground to a halt.

She was boring him, she knew, but there was nothing she could do about it. She was like the princess in the fairy story, only in her case it was not toads but monosyllables that leapt out every time she opened her mouth. Presently (and who could blame him?) he gave up, and stood lounging against the wall in silence, watching her drink her beer, waiting for her to finish.

How she got it down she did not know, it was so bitter, and such a lot of it, but she could hardly abandon it unfinished with him standing watching her like that through half-closed eyes. But she came to the end of it at last, and no sooner had she set the glass down than her companion seemed suddenly to spring to life. Seizing her by the elbow, he proceeded to steer her swiftly and purposefully through the crowd in the direction of the main doors.

"Let's get out of here!" he mouthed into her ear—the din by this time was terrible—and then, as the crowds began to thin out a little as they neared the exit, he added softly, "Feel like a stroll outside?"

CHAPTER 3

The moon was full, the air heavy with the scent of roses, but already, before he'd even kissed her, Miranda knew that it was over. She was in love no more. Somewhere during the course of this glittering long-awaited evening, between the moment when she'd entered the dance hall half faint with joy and this present moment of walking out under the moon arm in arm with the lover of her dreams—somewhere the glory had departed, and it would return no more.

In the grey of the moonlight, with the wet grass soaking up through her flimsy sandals, Miranda shivered a little; and her companion's arm tightened across her shoulders, just as it had done in so many a dream scenario.

What had happened? Where was the sense of a miracle come true? On the day I die, she should have been saying to herself, this is the moment I shall remember. This is the moment for which I was born, the moment for which all the rest of my life has been but a prelude, a background of shadow. Where *were* these longed-for, long-anticipated feelings?

If only it wasn't actually *happening*—that was what was spoiling it all! With a sort of desperation, like pushing her fist through a plate glass window, Miranda tried to reach right through and past the reality of it and get to the dream again; to clutch at those last wisps of magic which must—surely they must?—still be floating somewhere, just beyond her grasp, in the silvery light of the moon? This is *Trevor*, she kept insisting to herself . . . *Trevor Marks.*

Marks . . . Marks . . . the surname which only yesterday had set her heart thudding at the very sight of an L–R telephone directory? What had happened to the magic word? What ailed it? Why had it sickened thus in the pale light of the moon? With a gigantic effort of mental concentration, Miranda willed her heart to beat faster in the old wonderful way; but it would not.

And now, in the black moon-shadow of some great tree or something, he was kissing her. Kissing her "*like that*" as they were wont to describe it in the Fourth Form, and his tongue tasted exactly as you would have expected a tongue to taste. Which was odd, when you came to think about it, because how could she have had any expectations, never having tasted another person's tongue before? Once, in the childish times before they'd fallen in love, she and Sharon had discussed the matter at some length, and had decided—with some reluctance, indeed, but in the interests of research—to taste each other's tongues; but when it came to the point, the sight of one another's anxious faces looming nearer and nearer had reduced them to such a fit of giggling that the project had had to be abandoned.

They were in the shrubbery now, with hazel twigs and great flat clusters of rhododendron meeting above their heads. There was no wind, but the whole place was a-rustle with night sounds, and in the darkness silvery streaks of moonlight came at them like spears through the black leaves: and by now there was no doubt in Miranda's mind at all about what was going to happen. He was going to do "*It.*" This was another Fourth Form euphemism. His arms were like tight bands around her, and his voice was trembling.

"On the Pill, are you?" he asked hoarsely; and, "Yes!" lied Miranda without a moment's hesitation.

Well, you could hardly walk with a boy's arm around you all across a moonlit lawn and into a shrubbery, and then say "No," could you? Not nowadays, anyway. If you ever could, come to that, at any place or time?

Anyway, "Yes!" she answered stoutly—and then wondered, anxiously, what she was supposed to do next? *Did* the girl have to do anything, apart from saying "yes," or was it all up to the boy from this point on? This was something they didn't tell you in the sex lessons, and of course no one would dare to ask, because it would look as if they didn't know.

It seemed wrong, somehow, with most of their clothes still on like this, her pretty frothy skirt all bunched up around her waist and getting ruined. Somehow, she'd thought you were supposed to be naked; but Trevor had made no attempt to remove anything but his trousers, and of course he must know best. His weight was crushing; sharp twigs and spikey dead leaves left over from the winter were grinding into her shoulder blades through the nylon, but she dared not ask him to shift his position. Maybe the man couldn't, once he'd got started?—in which case it would be an awful request to make. Besides, she was supposed to be experiencing rapture, wasn't she, not thinking about twigs and things . . .

How *long* did it go on? That was another thing they didn't tell you in the sex lessons, didn't give you even the most approximate idea. Suppose it went on for an *hour!*

And there was another anxiety growing upon her as the moments passed: were you supposed to *talk* while it was going on? To make conversation? It had been bad enough trying to think up something to say while drinking beer with him, but this was much, much worse. What could you talk *about*, for heaven's sake? Nice evening, isn't it . . . ? Do you do this often . . . ?

Was it possible for the man to be actually *bored* while doing "It"? Was this why he wasn't saying anything, and had begun hurrying so . . . ?

And quite suddenly, it was over. It hadn't lasted an

hour or anything like it: more like a minute, really, or even less—and at first Miranda was uncertain whether it really *was* over? Suppose those little cries, this sudden collapse of movement, were a prelude to something further—something she ought to know about, that other girls knew about, and that he'd expect her know? How *did* you know for certain when the man was finished . . . ? Only when Trevor sat up, and began brushing twigs and leaves from his jacket, did she feel sure that the thing was really at an end, and ventured to sit up likewise.

In the darkness, she could hear him scrabbling his trousers back on, and she needed no silver shaft of moonlight to show her that he was avoiding looking in her direction.

Only when he was fully dressed and on his feet did he at last speak.

"Better go back separately," he muttered awkwardly. "I'll clear out right away, but don't you come . . . You wait here another couple of minutes . . ." and with a crash of undergrowth and snapping twigs he was gone.

There wasn't a reason in the world why they shouldn't have walked back across the moonlit lawn together, and he must have known it. The gardens were alive with strolling couples, no one would have given them a second glance. Sadly, Miranda fancied that she could see right through him to his real motives; that she understood, with her woman's intuition, the true nature of his reluctance.

He was bored with her. He'd been bored with her on the dance floor, bored during the stroll in the moonlight, bored during the sex act. Why should he inflict on himself the further boredom of escorting her back indoors?

"O.K.," she mumbled, utterly humbled by failure, and with no other thought in her mind other than so to comport herself as not to make matters even worse, to pile further humiliations on top of those already endured.

And never for one moment did it occur to her, either then or later, that he might be feeling just as bothered about the quality of his performance as she was about hers.

They had one thing in common, though, despite all these doubts and misunderstandings; and this was an urgent mutual need never to encounter one another again.

CHAPTER 4

"But, darling, if you love each other there's *nothing* to feel guilty about," urged Norah Field, leaning forward in her high-backed chair and gazing earnestly into her daughter's face. "Sex between young teenagers is *the* most *natural* thing . . . I can understand *exactly* how it happened . . ."

Understanding on this scale was only to be expected, of course, in a home like Miranda's; sitting there at her mother's feet, she felt it coming at her, wave after familiar wave.

"And I'm so *thankful,* darling," Mrs. Field continued, bending to stroke the bright, drooping head, "that you've come to *me* with your troubles, and not kept them hidden away . . . that you feel you can trust me . . . I'm so pleased about that—so very, *very* pleased . . . !"

She sounded pleased, too. Tracing with her forefinger the muted, pinkish patterns of the drawing room carpet, Miranda could not repress the suspicion that her mother was thoroughly enjoying herself. And why not, indeed? The whole thing was right up her street, she'd have been wasted, in a manner of speaking, on a daughter who *didn't* get pregnant while still in the Fourth Form.

"There's only just one thing, though, sweetheart"—Mrs. Field was hurrying through this bit as quickly as she could, anxious to get back to being non-judgemental at top speed—"just one thing I feel you've been a *teeny* bit naughty about. You should have told me, dear, as soon as —well, at the start of—I mean before the two of you actually . . . You see, if only I'd known, I could have had a word with the doctor, got him to fix you up with something . . ."

"He wouldn't have. I'm under-age," Miranda retorted, quite rudely; and for just a fraction of a second, Mrs. Field looked quite stunned, as if she'd been slapped across the face.

"Yes. Well . . ." She recovered herself. "And that's another thing dear. This boy. Of course, *I* know that it was all perfectly innocent and loving, on his side as well as yours, and of course I wouldn't dream—Daddy and I wouldn't *dream*—of doing anything to get him into any trouble—well, the police or anything, we wouldn't *dream* of it. But all the same, what he's done *is* a criminal offence. In the eyes of the silly old law, I mean. And so I do feel—if you could just bring yourself to tell us his name, in the most absolute and strictest confidence—after all, it *is* his baby too . . ."

"It's *not!* It's *my* baby!"

Miranda had leaped to her feet and was confronting her mother red-faced and hands on hips.

"It's *my* baby! It's *mine!* It's nothing to *do* with him, nothing whatever!" she shouted—a pronouncement so patently absurd that even Miranda herself could think of no way of following it up. With a defiant toss of the head, she turned on her heel and flung out of the room. She refrained, just in time, from slamming the door behind her. To bring Daddy in on it at this juncture, blinking worriedly behind his gold-rimmed spectacles and trying feebly to be as progressive as Mummy—this would have been just about the last straw.

Lying on her bed, eyes shaded against the blaze of the summer evening through the open windows, Miranda found her anger cooling. What had possessed her to be so rude and horrid, when Mummy was being as kind and nice about it all as any mother could possibly be? Why couldn't she respond with gratitude and appreciation instead of with sulks and rudeness—not to mention stupid and irrational back-answering?

Irrational, perhaps. But stupid? Miranda closed her eyes against the glory of the sunset, deeply pondering. Had there not been a kind of truth in her wildly illogical declaration—a truth that lay beyond logic? There was a sense, explicable to no one but herself, in which the baby *was* nothing to do with Trevor. The encounter had been too brief, too trivial, too disappointing, to have had any part in so mighty a consequence. The whole thing had lasted barely a minute, and seemed, in retrospect, so unimportant, so devoid of meaning. Having once got over the sense of failure, the feelings of shame at her own ineptitude in the sex act, it was the *triviality* of the whole experience which had amazed her most; its total lack of significance. Here she was, a virgin no longer, the mysterious hurdle surmounted, the legendary Rubicon crossed—and *nothing was changed!* She felt the same. She looked the same. Back in the cloakroom, she'd run a comb through her hair, straightened her rucked-up skirt, and gone back to the dance as if nothing had happened. By morning, even the slight soreness and the faint achey feeling were gone. No trace of bodily disturbance, no upheaval of the soul, no flicker of unaccustomed sensation of any kind, gave warning of the mighty changes that had been set in motion. And even a fortnight later, her period already six days overdue and her breasts tingling strangely, she still could not take in what was happening.

It was not that she had failed to notice the symptoms, or was unaware of their significance: it was just that the whole thing was impossible to believe in, like a fairy story. That a hurried and graceless entangling of limbs and genitals, lasting a minute or less, should have consequences vast and incalculable, stretching on and on into the unimaginable future—it was beyond all comprehending. As a result of that single inconsequential minute, a new and perfectly formed living creature was destined to walk the earth, to breathe the air, to feel the heat of the sun, for seventy or eighty years . . . Easier, far, to believe that the Doctor would bring the baby in his black bag, that a stork would swoop down with it out of the bright air.

Yet truth it was. It was a scientific fact. Those passing moments of embarrassment and disillusion had been sublime moments of creation. The imagination could not register so incongruous a causal sequence, nor belief encompass it.

But as the days went by—seven . . . eight . . . nine, and still her period hadn't come, belief began, almost imperceptibly to establish itself in her consciousness. It came not suddenly, in a flash of revelation, but in a slow, unstoppable tide of growing wonder, of half-incredulous joy.

A baby! I'm having a *baby!* I, Miranda Field, schoolgirl, have been vouchsafed this miracle of new life growing inside me! I'm pregnant! *Me!* It's happening to *me!*

There had been occasions, in the long-ago time before all this had happened, when she and Sharon had indulged in fantasies of Virgin Births, and man-less pregnancies. They had discussed, with much giggling and yet half-credulously, the likelihood or otherwise of being impregnated while they slept by the Holy Ghost: what it would feel like? and whether they'd still remember it in the morning . . . ?

An immaculate conception! Strange how childish fantasies can so truly foreshadow the realities to come! For this was exactly what it felt like—as if the glory that had come upon her had its origin in some sacred source beyond human understanding, far, far removed from Trevor with his heavy gasping and his offhand, uneasy haste . . .

It was *real!* It was happening! To *her!* Lying here on her rumpled bed, in her familiar childhood bedroom, the miracle was already beginning. Inside her, right now, as she lay here, a little creature no bigger than a frog was forming limbs for itself, and eyes, and the beginnings of a brain; a brain which would one day contain a vocabulary of forty or fifty thousand words, as well as geometry, and algebra, and the names and addresses of countless friends and acquaintances yet unborn. At this very moment, only an inch or two below her knicker elastic, those first clusters of cells were gathering in readiness to read Shakespeare, to listen to Beethoven and Elvis Presley, to learn "On Westminster Bridge" by heart; to gaze through a telescope at the moons of Jupiter, to read about black holes, and wonder about the infinite spaces beyond the furthest galaxies . . .

"Darling . . . ! I'm so sorry I upset you, I didn't mean . . ."

But it was *she*, Miranda, who should be apologising, not Mummy! It wasn't *fair!* Mummy always managed to get the better of you, somehow! Swivelling round onto her stomach, Miranda buried her face in the pillow, and lay there, mute and ashamed, waiting for it all to be over.

And yet still Mummy kept hovering there between the bed and the door, baffled and uncondemning, poised as on a tightrope between staying and going, and babbling uneasily on and on about misunderstandings, and about it being nearly dinner-time, and about not worrying Daddy just now, with the by-election coming on, and about nobody blaming anybody for anything, and was Miranda not feeling well, would she like some nice hot soup on a tray, in bed . . . ?

If Mrs. Field had been one of those straight-laced, censorious parents she so despised, actually *trying* to make her daughter feel guilty and awful, she couldn't have made a better job of it. Miranda pulled the eiderdown over her head and buried her face deeper in the pillow; and when, a few minutes later, she ventured warily to peep out, her mother was gone.

Presently, a delicious smell of oxtail, cooked with thyme and bayleaves, began to float upstairs.

Her favourite meal! Had Mummy done it on purpose, to make her feel even more churlish and ungrateful? Or (let's be fair) had she done it lovingly, to cheer her up, and make her feel cherished?

Either way, there was the same decision to be made: sulks or supper? No one can reasonably expect both, and so after a brief struggle between the flesh and the spirit, Miranda rolled off the bed, combed her hair, slid her feet into her slip-slop sandals, and went downstairs to the dining room.

Daddy had already been told, obviously. He was wearing his see-no-evil, hear-no-evil look which he never ceased to hope would somehow make things not have happened. And indeed, it worked well enough at Ward Labour Party meetings quite often, but less well at home.

On this occasion, the better not to see what was going on, he had taken his glasses off as well (he was shortsighted) and laid them by his plate, so that the bluish fuzz now materialising in the doorway bore but a minimal resemblance to anyone's daughter, let alone his own, in blue-and-white checked shirt and faded jeans, carrying Trouble towards his dinner table like a loaded tray . . .

"Hello, Daddy," Miranda greeted him, brightly and deliberately—the transparency of his evasion tactics always irritated her, wasn't he supposed to have an I.Q. of 140, or something?—"I'm having a baby, did Mummy tell you?" she continued chattily, pulling out her chair and sitting down at the table, "around the beginning of March—"

"Hush, dear! Not just now!" her mother admonished in an urgent undertone, while her father made a brave effort to choke on a forkful of mashed potato, and then to hear the telephone ringing out in the silent hall. Twice he rushed headlong to answer this phantom summons; and by the time he'd returned the second time, the conversation had sure enough moved into safer channels, and he was able to finish his meal in peace.

The ostrich, burying his head in the sand, has long been a laughing stock; but all the same, it really can work. After all, if it couldn't, ostriches would have been out of the evolutionary stream long ago, and so, presumably, would people like Edwin Field. The Survival of the Fittest manifests itself in diverse and sometimes surprising ways—look at the toucan, for example, or the duck-billed platypus.

Sooner or later, of course, Mrs. Field would pin him down and force him to face the facts, but by that time the worst would be over, and she would be in a position to tell him what he should think and, if there was anything he ought to do, to make him do it. Such had been her benign practice over all these years, and there seemed no good reason why any drastically different system should suddenly be put into operation now.

By the time the meal was over, and she'd gone back upstairs, Miranda's room was bathed in pinkish light, and the bright cotton curtains that Mummy had made her for her thirteenth birthday were stirring gently in the cool of the evening. In the far corner of the room, dusty, unloved, and neglected these five or six years, Miranda's old doll's house was flashing with sparks of rosy light from its tiny lattice windows, long unopened.

How she had loved that doll's house once! And what a nuisance it had been ever since, remorselessly continuing to exist, gathering dust, blocking up that useful alcove, and yet somehow quietly and inexplicably resisting every decision to give it away to this or that deserving child, or on behalf of this, that or the other worthy cause.

Miranda hadn't looked at the thing except with mild and helpless irritation for years, but suddenly this evening she found herself noticing all over again how pretty it was—how enchanting, really, all aglow in the last rays of the sunset, and the little windows shining just as they used to shine when she polished them with that inch-square of wash-leather that Mummy had snipped off for her that rainy afternoon six—seven?—years ago. There'd been a tiny bucket, too, and a ladder made from match sticks glued to cardboard struts, for Grandfather to climb up on his stiff, unyielding plastic legs.

What fun it had been! Crouching down in front of her old treasure, Miranda manoeuvred open the absurd little front door (it had always been inclined to stick, and now it was worse than ever from disuse), and peered into the dark little hallway, still carpeted with those scraps of maroon corduroy left over from the pinafore dress Mummy had made her one winter holidays, when she was about eight. The little stairs were carpeted likewise, boasting even stair rods made from wooden toothpicks, laboriously halved with blunt (and subsequently quite useless) scissors.

On to the ornate, ridiculous dining room, crammed with match-box furniture, and lumpy, impossible sets of dining chairs (even a doll couldn't balance on them) made from conkers stuck with pins. How well she recalled Mummy showing her how to make them . . . and the wonderful, golden October afternoon when they'd collected the conkers, gleaming like polished mahogany through the cracks in the green, spikey rind . . .

And in the midst of it all, decrepit and unloved, there lay in a dusty little heap the whole Mactaggerty family—Grandfather Mactaggerty, with his white beard come unglued and dangling round his left ear and his stick all out sideways . . . Grandmother Mactaggerty eternally smiling down—even now, with her legs in the air—at the knitting stitched permanently to her lap, Mummy Mactaggerty, Daddy Mactaggerty and the three naughty little Mactaggerty children, Rosalinda, Rosamunda, and (for some reason she could not recall) French, his perky, bell-bottomed trousers tattered and dusty now beyond all recognition.

How the baby was going to love them! Little though they knew it, their days of loveless retirement were coming to an end, and life would begin for them again. Soon, there would be new little fingers to set Grandfather's beard straight for him again, and to send him—*hobb*ledy-hop, *hobb*ledy-hop—out shopping. Or to the office. Or up in an aeroplane. In a year—well, no, two years—the Mactaggerty's would be on their feet again, having fun again, adventures again, and raisins, and crumbs of chocolate biscuit on the tiny plates . . . .

That her baby would be a girl, Miranda had never doubted. Already she had decided to call her Caroline. Like "Caroline and her Seaside Friends"—and after Granny, too, of course. Granny would have been awfully pleased . . .

Would she, in view of all the circumstances? The wishes of the dead are, of course, difficult to ascertain, but it is surprising, in practice, how often their opinions turn out to be just what is maximally convenient for their survivors; and why should Miranda's Granny be an exception to this rule?

Dusk was falling, the inside of the doll's house was thick with shadows. Reaching with her giant, overgrown fist into the dining room, Miranda gathered up the Mactaggertys in a single handful and carried them over to the desk to look at them properly under the reading lamp. To look at them, that is, through Caroline's fresh, wondering eyes, already in the process of coming into being.

They were awful! Well, not *them*, not the Mactaggertys themselves, for they were indestructible—but their *clothes!*

Dirty, tattered, cobbled together with huge, uneven stitches, and not even hemmed, half of them—had she really been such a rotten needlewoman at the ripe age of nine? Or even ten, was it? She couldn't possibly pass them on to Baby Caroline in such a state. It might well put her right off them, and would certainly spoil the magic moment of the presentation. Something would have to be done.

And this was why, an hour or two later, under the soft drawing room lights, "What *are* you making, dear?" Mummy had asked, peering, puzzled, at the tiny scrap of red-and-white check gingham at which Miranda was busily stitching.

"It's Rosalinda's new frock, Mummy," Miranda explained, proudly and a little shyly. "You remember Rosalinda, don't you—one of my dolls? I'm refurbishing the doll's house, you see, ready for Caroline—for the baby—that is . . ."

Her voice faltered into silence, for a most extraordinary thing was happening. So sympathetic, so almost preternaturally understanding Mummy had been until this moment—and now, suddenly her eyes were hard and angry, her voice shrill.

"Ridiculous! Throw it away at once! Really, I don't know how you can be so childish! As if there were nothing more to worry about than . . . *Miranda!* Did you hear me? I said, *Throw it away!* At once!" And Miranda, utterly taken aback, too startled to protest, obediently tossed the absurd little object into the wastepaper basket, and sat staring up at her mother, uncomprehending and speechless.

Later, Mummy was sorry. Really sorry.

"I didn't mean to upset you, darling," she pleaded, for the second time that day, "but you see"—here her voice quivered, almost as if she was on the verge of tears—"oh, darling, I'm only trying to do my best for you! You know that, don't you? I want to help you, sweetheart, in every way I possibly can. I'll do anything . . . *anything!* Surely you know that . . . ?"

And Miranda did know it. Of course she did. They hugged one another, even wept a little, in sheer relief.

CHAPTER 5

By mid-July, Miranda was the heroine of the Fourth Year. Awed whispers and envious or incredulous glances followed her wherever she went: her peregrinations between playground and classroom, between chemistry lab and music rooms, took on the nature of a royal progress, heads popping from windows all along the route, and furtive little crowds gathering to watch and whisper as she passed by.

Pregnant? Miranda Field? You've got to be joking! No, but really, no kidding! She told Sharon herself, and Sharon told me! Or Angela told me . . . or Vanessa told me . . . or Judith . . . or Doreen . . . the qualified informants by now were legion.

It must be like this to be an astronaut, or a pop star. During those last days of the summer term, Miranda basked in such glory as she had never known, eclipsing effortlessly and completely the erstwhile radiance of those once-envied girls who had merely had "*It.*"

A *baby!* Miranda Field going to have a *baby* . . . ! The nine days' wonder of it seemed as if it would never end. In the slow, windless heat of late July, with exams over and with the school year grinding gently to its close, the Miranda Field drama expanded to fill the minds available for its contemplation.

"Tell us what it's *like!*" her wide-eyed audience would plead, in hushed tones, awed in the presence of such immensity of experience. Can you feel it moving yet? Is it like—well, like a sort of *lump* inside you? Well, what *is* it like, then? Do you feel sick at all? Not morning sickness or anything? Do you have weird cravings, like for raw parsnips and things? Or *coal?* Someone's sister—or was it —someone's sister's friend?—had had this awful craving for coal, great shiny lumps of it, she'd be scrunching them up all evening, her saliva all black all the time, so that in the end her husband . . . Does it *show* at all, when you've got nothing on? Do you have to wear anything special—you know—underneath? Are you beginning to have peculiar dreams . . . ?

Tell us! Tell us! The eternal cry of Life's stay-at-homes to the voyager from far places—but how to answer it? How to convey to them—to anyone—the sense of holiness that enfolded her; the feeling of having been chosen, of moving like a priestess, robed in splendour, towards some shining altar on which the whole of the future lay curled and waiting? She, Miranda Field, was part of evolution now, a member of the evolutionary elite who have been selected-in, and whose genes are to pass into immortality . . .

"Miranda! Miranda Field! This is the *second* time I've had to speak to you this afternoon! Now, will you kindly answer my questions: When the Council of Fourteen finally resolved to put their case before the King, why was it that . . ."

The Council of Fourteen. Fourteen strong men, fully grown, and every one of them must have started with a missed period! Every one of them must have grown from tiny, tadpole-like beginnings in some long-dead womb, which had thrust them headlong into history, so that now here they were, four hundred years later, on an O-Level syllabus of which they could never have dreamed . . .

"Really, Miranda! You seem half asleep these days! You'll have to do better than this next year, you know, if you're to—Oh, all right, then, Julia, *you* tell us . . ."

Two and a half inches long now! Right here, under the waistband of her school skirt, and the fingers beginning to form, with tiny nails . . . The wonder of it swept over her like a great wind, her consciousness billowing out before it, and filling her with a sense of her own power, her own wisdom, her own unimaginable skills. Not so much as an eyelash would she know consciously how to create, and yet here was this body of hers—*her own body,* her very self—knowing—easily, effortlessly knowing—exactly how to make a whole new human being, perfect in every detail. No biologist in all the world, with all the techniques of all the research departments on the whole earth at his disposal, could do what she could do. Hers was the secret of life; and here, at an ordinary desk, in a drowsy afternoon classroom with a boring history lesson going on, was its dwelling place. Here, with Miss Fergusson's voice droning in her ears, she sat among the immortals, carrying within her the answer to it all.

Tell us! . . . Tell us . . . ! When the lesson was over, and the books being packed away, the questions once again rose twittering all around her, like flocks of small birds arising from freshly tilled ploughland; and as always, she tried honestly to answer them.

But it was no use. The harder she tried, the more it sounded like one of those spirit messages that come through at a seance: It's so beautiful . . . so wonderful . . . I can't explain, but it's all so beautiful . . . everyone's so happy here . . .

"Sounds plain daft to me," remarked Doreen Briggs, sturdy and down-to-earth, and not troubling to disguise the scorn in her voice. "I mean, what are you going to *do* with a baby, Miranda? At your age, I mean, and not married or anything! It's daft! And what's your mum going to say?"

"My mother's being marvellous about it," retorted Miranda loftily. "And so is my father," she added, as a dutiful afterthought, and probably with a substantial element of truth; after all, being marvellous is often a good deal less trouble than arguing. "I've told them everything," she finished smugly, "and they're going to help me with the baby every way they can."

Doreen sniffed incredulously.

"Daft," she repeated unrepentantly. "If they've any sense, they'll make you get rid of it!"

And it was only three days later, over iced tea with slices of lemon in it on the sunny lawn, that she learned that this was exactly what her parents planned to do.

CHAPTER 6

"So you *see,* darling, *all* we're thinking of is what'll be best for *you,"* Mrs. Field was desperately explaining, stabbing nervously at her words as she always did when limbering up for a major confrontation. "We've talked and *talked* about it, Daddy and I, we've gone over *every* possibility, and we've come to the conclusion that the *only* thing . . ."

"I won't! I'm not going to! I'm not interested in your beastly, horrible conclusions, it's nothing to *do* with you, or Daddy either! It's *my* baby, and it's *my* decision; and I've told you, I won't! I just won't! You can't make me . . ."

Or could they? This was the tiny, agonising niggle of doubt gnawing away at the soft, quivering underside of Miranda's brave words. *Was* it possible, if you were under-age, for your parents to drag you kicking and screaming to the hospital for what they considered to be a necessary operation? Had they the power, while nurses and orderlies held you down, to sign the necessary forms on your behalf? And would the surgeon, on their signed say-so, be entitled to wreak their parental will on your helpless, adolescent body regardless of your shrieks and pleadings? Would it be his right—his duty even—to commit this outrage at the behest of your legal guardians? But even if this was the case, would any surgeon, in practice, actually do it? Or would he—duty or no—refuse to operate in such circumstances? It wouldn't be a pretty scene, with the patient fighting him every inch of the way, screaming and pleading for her baby's life, twisting her head this way and that, holding her breath against the anaesthetic . . .

Would he? Could he? Were there some surgeons who would go ahead regardless . . . others who would refuse to do so? Were you thus completely at the mercy of their clinical whims? And if you were, then what would be the best way to win them over to your side? Maybe screaming and fighting would, after all, be counterproductive, serving merely to convince them—exchanging knowing, adult glances above your frantic head—that you were indeed just as childish, hysterical, and unfit for the responsibilities of motherhood as your parents had claimed you were . . . ?

What *were* your legal rights when you were only fifteen? You must have some—but how to discover them? And, above all, to discover them in time . . .

To do Mummy justice, she hadn't for one moment threatened Miranda with her and Daddy's legal powers—not so far, anyway. For the time being, sweet reason was Mrs. Field's preferred suit, and she was playing it for all it was worth.

A *baby*? At *fifteen*? Surely Miranda could see for herself what a catastrophe it would be? How it would wreck her whole life at the very outset, all hopes of a proper education, a proper career, and a happy successful future at the end? There would be no hope any more of Miranda's getting into University, which was what they'd always planned for her, bright, clever girl that she was; or of qualifying for an interesting, creative job commensurate with her talents. It would be wicked, it would be an outrage, to allow her to throw away all these chances right at the start, before she was old enough to know what she was doing! And her chances of a happy marriage one of these days—those, too, would go by the board: who did she suppose would want to marry a girl burdened with another man's child before she'd even reached the age of consent?

And think, too (Norah Field's voice began to take on an almost wheedling note)—think, too, of all the *fun* she'd be missing, the lovely carefree years of the late teens and early twenties which are every girl's birthright! How did she think she'd feel in two or three years' time, when all her friends were going out into the world, travelling, meeting new people, having adventures, falling in love—while she, Miranda was stuck at home night after night, year after year, serving her life sentence of baby-sitting?

It just didn't bear thinking of! And all the time, the solution was staring them in the face—just a quick and very nearly painless visit to the hospital—hardly anything more than a visit to the dentist—and back home in a day or so, right as rain.

"You don't know how *lucky* you are, in your generation!" Mrs. Field admonished, "having it all so easy and above board, and with no stigma attached! When *I* was your age, a nasty, dangerous back-street abortion would have been the only option . . . some awful old woman with a knitting needle, most likely . . . and all the time terrified of being found out because you knew that what you were doing was illegal . . ."

"I'd *love* to have lived in those days!" burst out Miranda furiously. "If it was an awful old woman with a knitting needle, then you couldn't *make* me go to her, you'd be breaking the law, I could demand police protection, I could get you put in prison!"

The quarrel was beginning to escalate beyond either of their control; it was frightening, and yet there seemed nowhere to go but on.

"Miranda! What a terrible thing to say! And anyway, no one's talking about *making* you do anything! I'm not for one moment trying to impose my will on you—it's just that you surely must see for yourself . . ."

But Miranda didn't see. Wouldn't see. Couldn't see. She

was fighting for her baby's life, and could see nothing beyond.

"I won't," she kept repeating doggedly. "I just won't. I'm not going to. I've told you, I'm *not going to.*"

So far Mrs. Field had been trying, with ever-increasing desperation, to keep the argument on an enlightened, rational plane, and encourage her daughter to come to her own decisions in a mature and rational way. But what can you do with a person who, instead of coming to mature and rational decisions, just keeps saying "I won't!"? How can you maintain a permissive, non-judgemental, open-minded attitude towards people who just won't see sense? After all, the Permissive Society can hardly be expected to cater for the sort of people who flatly refuse to do the things it permits.

"Really, Miranda! Do we *have* to go on and on like this, the same arguments over and over again, and never getting anywhere! It's so *boring*, as well as stupid! And such a waste of time! And *time*, you know, dear, is something we just can't *afford* to waste, not any longer. You see, it's so *very* important—and if you don't believe me, ask any doctor—so *very* important not to let it go beyond three months because by then it'll be too big. You see, after that . . ."

"She's *not* 'it'!" Miranda choked out, tears of fury once again filling eyes worn red with the long afternoon's weeping. "She's *Caroline!* She—"

"Oh, but darling, that's where you're so *silly*, talking like that!" cried Mrs. Field. "It's ridiculous! 'Caroline' indeed—and you don't even know yet if it's a boy or a girl! And actually it isn't either, not yet: it's just a nothing . . . a blob of jelly . . ."

"She's *not!*"

"I'm sorry, darling, but it *is*, and that's a fact! Don't you realise it's still only . . ."

It isn't! It is! It isn't! Don't shout at me like that! I'm *not* shouting! You *are* shouting! I'm not . . . ! you are . . . ! I'm not! Darling—*Please*—the *neighbours!* The neighbours, the neighbours, that's all you care about, you and Daddy, what the neighbours will think! And you supposed to be so left-wing, both of you . . . so modern and progressive . . . and now, when it comes to the crunch! . . . Hush, dear, oh *please* hush! Everyone all down the street . . .

The mother pleaded: the daughter grew ever more defiant. I won't, she continued to assert, obstinately, sullenly, and doggedly. I won't. I'm not going to. I don't care what you do, you can tear me with wild horses, I'll never give in!

In the event, wild horses proved to be unnecessary. The power of emotional blackmail should not, after all, be underestimated, nor the slow wearing down of the spirit over many days. On Tuesday, August 3, at 10:30 A.M., white and silent, eyes swollen with crying, but without protest, Miranda climbed obediently onto the surgeon's couch and submitted herself to the operation.

Baby Caroline would never know, now, what it was like to be more than three inches long, this was as big as she would ever be. Those half-formed, bulbous eyes would never see, nor the ears hear. The sprouting fingers, with their tiny fingernails already forming, would never now play the piano, whip up an omelette, or hold a pen. Like buds shrivelled by the frosts of a late, cold spring, their tiny day was over.

CHAPTER 7

Perhaps it would have been better if they *had* threatened her with wild horses, or some similarly heroic ordeal. To be forced by sheer physical violence into submission may leave scars on the body, but the soul, with any luck, can soar above it unscathed. If Miranda had fought, as she had planned to fight, with teeth and nails against a steely-eyed robot of a surgeon, whose response to her screams and pleadings was merely to summon four muscular orderlies to hold her down—had this been the scene, then she might have emerged from it with her spirit unbroken; vanquished indeed, but with some shreds of self-respect to sustain her through the ensuing days of grief and loss.

But that's not the way it was at all. They couldn't have been nicer, all of them, from the young, smiling surgeon who talked to her so soothingly and reassuringly while he examined her before the operation, to the pretty, kind-hearted nurses who greeted her return to consciousness in a bright, sunny room full of flowers. A private room, apparently. "Real V.I.P. treatment!" as one of the young nurses laughingly put it, remarking on what a lucky girl Miranda was to have parents who cared so much about her welfare as to pay for private treatment. "Nothing but the best good enough for *their* daughter!" the girl summed it up, half admiring and half critical. "And getting you to the top of the list, too!—there's girls nearly four months gone and still waiting, to my certain knowledge . . . *Somebody's* Dad knows how to pull the strings, that's for sure . . ."

It would have been Mummy, of course, not Daddy, who would have pulled the strings—or, rather, would have guided his hand while he did it, making sure that he deployed to best advantage his contacts both at work and in politics. Mummy was marvellous at this sort of thing. She must be loving it.

And as a result of all this, the whole affair had gone off splendidly; everything turned out exactly as Miranda had been promised it would. As far as physical pain was concerned, it really had been "no more than a visit to the dentist"—less, if anything; and by the end of the day she really was feeling "as right as rain." The young surgeon, visiting in the late afternoon, was delighted with her—regular pulse, no disquieting fluctuations of temperature or blood pressure, no complications of any kind. Like most doctors, he found it quite a treat to be dealing, now and again, with a perfectly healthy body in peak condition and with absolutely nothing wrong with it. Among all the fibroids, prolapses, and hysterectomies of his gynaecological practice, this sort of thing was quite a little oasis in his day.

And of course, from his point of view, it was an open-and-shut case—the perfect, archetypal situation for which the more liberal abortion laws of the past decade had been expressly designed: a young teenager, still at school, getting herself pregnant after a few drinks, by a boy she scarcely knew and with whom she'd had no contact since —this was just the sort of case to which abortion was the humane and obvious answer. Fortunately the parents weren't Catholic or anything, there were no complicated religious scruples to be got round, nor were they the guilt-ridden old-fashioned types who were against the easy way out on principle. In fact, they seemed to be a singularly enlightened couple, remarkably free of the sort of hang-ups typical of their generation, and thus able to come to a balanced, sensible decision, their daughter's welfare the only consideration. If only all parents were like these!

The girl herself had seemed a bit quiet and tearful; but then this was by no means uncommon, and when you considered what these girls had usually been through in the preceding weeks—family rows, perhaps, and anxieties and humiliations of all kinds—you couldn't wonder. To see the way they perked up when the op. was safely over, to witness the relief and gratitude on the young faces when they woke to their new freedom, their new lease of carefree living—this was what made the job so worth-while.

Not that "perked up" was quite the phrase that best described this latest patient of his when he paused, smiling, at her bedside. She was still subdued and monosyllabic, though physically (as he quickly and expertly ascertained) in tip-top condition: good colour, regular pulse, everything exactly as it should be.

"My prize patient!" he tried to jolly her up, "I wish they all looked like you three hours after leaving the theatre! Any pain anywhere? Any headache? Any problems with passing water?"

He knew there wouldn't be; he was far too good a surgeon for bungled side effects of this nature to be a feature of his post-operative rounds; and so, "Good girl, you'll be fighting fit by the weekend!" he encouraged her, smiling down into the wide, unblinking eyes fixed on his own, "and this time watch your step a bit, eh, young lady?"—and with a friendly pat on her shoulder, he was gone.

To have let off her rage, her grief, and her despair into that kindly, unsuspecting face would have been unthinkable. Besides, the thing was done now, and couldn't be undone. And even this morning, when the options, in theory, were still open, the practical impossibility of making any sort of last-ditch stand against the calm and ordered structure of events in a well-run hospital, was something that had caught her completely by surprise. To have turned upon all these kind, committed people, who had gone to such trouble to fit her into their busy schedule, to repay their concern and sympathy with shrieks of rage and ingratitude: to have fought off with kicks and blows those gentle, ministering hands: to have clawed with her sharp nails at that pleasant, boyish face as it leaned over her so eager to comfort and reassure—it would have been impossible. How could she have known that *these* would be the enemies, and that the weapons she'd been secretly, silently sharpening against them through the long nights of sleepless fury, would suddenly be limp in her hands, like toy daggers, cut out of cardboard, and left all night in the rain?

Rather than make an undignified and shocking scene, rather than affront and appal all these pleasant, well-behaved, well-intentioned experts, rather than disgrace herself in public, she had allowed Baby Caroline to die.

It was no good hating them. They had only been doing their job. For her remaining hours in hospital, Miranda's behaviour was quiet and unremarkable. She ate little, but answered politely when they spoke to her, said Yes, thank you, she was feeling fine.

Hating was for when she got home.

Mummy couldn't possibly have been kinder or more loving. During the two days after Miranda left hospital, Mrs. Field devoted herself totally to her daughter's comfort and well-being, cosseting and fussing over her as if she were a little girl again suffering from some minor childhood illness, bringing her cool drinks, and trays of delicious food—even offering to read aloud to her, and to play card games, as in days gone by. If Mrs. Field was aware of the waves of silent hostility and rejection that met her every overture, she gave no sign of it: Miranda's monosyllabic rudeness was put down to "the strain of it all, poor child!" and her sullen silences to "hormonal readjustment—only to be expected!"

On the third evening, Daddy was brought in on the act. One on each side of her bed, in the last of the evening sunshine, the motes weaving back and forth between the two pale faces in the shafts of dying light, they sat like two effigies attendant on a medieval tomb.

They were telling her—or, rather, Mummy was telling her, with Daddy nodding, and polishing his glasses, and making little noises of assent while furtively glancing at his watch—about the lovely, lovely holiday they were going to have, a real family holiday, as soon as Miranda was quite recovered. Sicily . . . Tangiers . . . Morocco . . . it was going to be the holiday of a lifetime: warm seas, hot sunshine, exotic foreign food, and dancing in tavernas far into the night . . .

It was reminiscent of a funeral service for someone who has died in not very creditable circumstances: the hushed, uneasy evocation of bliss to come, combined with a careful avoidance of any reference to the unfortunate goings-on that had led to the demise; and all this against a background of overpowering scent from the roses with which Mummy, in a frenzy of conciliation, had filled her daughter's bedroom. What with one thing and another, Miranda felt that she was lying on her own bier, all the formalities of death completed except only for oblivion, which had somehow, in the press of funeral arrangements, been overlooked.

I hate them. I hate them. I hate them! I'll never forgive them: never! With eyes downcast, Miranda allowed the gruesome travelogue of sea and sky to flow round and past her, and spoke never a word in answer.

"And of course you'll need lots of new clothes, darling," Mrs. Field was continuing, bright and indomitable as ever, and embarked straight away on a dazzling list of all the crisp sun dresses, all the expensive tailored slacks and the stylish bikinis with which she proposed to pay for the death of Baby Caroline.

I hate you. I hate you. I hate you. I'll die in the gutter before I'll go with you on your grisly, murderous holiday, before I'll wear a stitch of clothing bought with your bloodstained conscience money!

If only she'd dared to say it aloud! Where was she now, the proud girl who had flung defiance across the summer lawn, head held high, eyes blazing?—the girl whom even wild horses couldn't subdue?

Ah, where was she? Defeated, broken, traitor to her own true self as well as to her child: a craven, vanquished thing, without courage, without pride. She hadn't even the nerve, now, to say so much as "I'm sorry, I don't want to go."

"And *perhaps,*" Mrs. Field was concluding, with the bright panicky optimism of a conjurer scrabbing for a last rabbit in a final, desperate hat, "*perhaps,* if he's home in time, Sam could come, too? It's years since we've had a holiday all together, all four of us. Or maybe we could meet him somewhere en route—wouldn't that be fun?"

Fun it would *not* be, nor ever could have been, even in circumstances far more propitious than these. Fond though she was of her older brother, Miranda had often found herself wondering why it was that her parents could not accept, once and for all, that deeply though they loved their now grown-up son, they simply could not stand his company. Hadn't been able to for years. He'd been such a disappointment to them, for one thing—and such a poor advertisement, too, for the painstakingly enlightened methods by which they'd brought him up. They'd had to stand by and watch first one and then another of his contemporaries—products, quite often, of broken marriages, corporal punishment, rigid authoritarianism, the lot—watch them one after another sailing successfully through University, landing good jobs, forming stable relationships, while all the time here was Sam continuing mildly but inexorably a disgrace to them.

Not that Sam had ever done anything so very dreadful: it was more the things he *hadn't* done. Hadn't finished his homework ever; hadn't gone in for any creative hobbies; hadn't practised on the expensive violin they'd bought him; hadn't done well enough in A-levels to warrant applying to Oxford or Cambridge; hadn't even filled in his UCCA forms properly. And when, finally, he'd arrived at his not very prestigious University, he hadn't stayed there. Even his dropping out hadn't been a positive act of defiance; he hadn't marched out in mid-term as gesture of protest against something or other, shaking the dust of the place off his feet; rather, he had simply failed to return at the end of one Easter vacation, had failed, if the truth must be told, to wake up in time to catch the right train.

From then on, the things that Sam hadn't done were as the sands of the sea. He hadn't applied for any proper jobs, attended any courses, or even found himself a nice steady girlfriend; and on top of everything else, he had made not the smallest attempt to get away from home and lead a life of his own. He had seemed perfectly content to remain in his parents' house, lying in bed till midday, playing pop records, and conducting singularly labour-saving love affairs with such girls as happened along. And when, in a last desperate attempt to get him to lead a life of his own, Mr. and Mrs. Field had had the top floor of their house converted into a self-contained flat for him, he had taken neither pride nor interest in his new domain, letting it go to rack and ruin, never tidying it, never cleaning it, and never even cooking anything much in the spanking new little kitchenette; preferring to bring home take-away meals from the local Kebab House, and to eat them in front of his parents' television, just as he had always done, leaving a trail of greasy plastic containers all over the drawing room. Occasionally, when a more than usually domesticated girl happened to have floated within his range, things would be different for a few weeks. The flat would burst into sudden hectic life, pans of burnt rice left soaking in the little sink, and all the woodwork suddenly daubed with orange (or Prussian blue, as the case might be) emulsion paint, splinters, rusty nails and all; and yet another batch of gallon paint cans (bought wholesale, for economy's sake) would stand with their lids off on the little landing, gently drying up in company with yet another set of brand-new paint brushes, standing caked with paint in a jar of dried-up turpentine.

No, there was no harm in Sam; as older brothers go, he wasn't bad at all. Miranda had always found him kind enough, and quite fun to have around. She had long ago formed the opinion that his failings, many and various though they might appear, were really only one failing: he couldn't stand bother.

And yet, this couldn't be the whole answer either, because hitch-hiking overland to India must surely be a bother, by any standards; and this was the adventure from which he was expected home some time during the next few weeks.

The daylight was nearly gone now, and as dusk gathered in her pretty flower-filled bedroom, Miranda pretended to have fallen asleep, her eyelids closed in apparent tranquillity over the hatred, rage, and misery that seethed beneath. She heard her mother's bright, strained voice faltering at last into hopelessness; and then, a little later, she heard the two of them tiptoeing furtively from the room. Presently, the familiar evening sounds of the household sank likewise into silence; and now, at last, Miranda crept softly out of bed and tiptoed across the room.

It was hard to decide what, if anything, to take with

her; hard, even, to decide what to wear for the journey. What sort of travelling outfit *is* the right one for a future stretching bare and featureless as a desert into the unimaginable distance?

"You'll need lots of new clothes!" Mrs. Field had declared, with manic, desperate optimism: and all the time, right here in Miranda's wradrobe, *were* the new clothes she should have been needing, never yet worn: two very pretty and becoming maternity smocks, bought with her birthday money when she became fifteen only a couple of weeks ago.

So practical had these purchases seemed at the time, as well as exciting and delightful, because although it was early days yet, she *would* be needing them before winter set in. She had been quite unprepared for the little gasp of horror her mother had been unable to suppress at the sight of them.

Now, she understood it only too well. Already, Mummy had known that the garments would never be worn, that no maternity clothes would ever be required. Even on that first evening, when the two of them had clung together in such apparent closeness and love, the decision must already have been quietly taken . . .

It was easier, somehow, to write it down than it had been to say it out loud.

"I hate you," Miranda wrote, neatly and carefully, bending over her desk in the little circle of rosy light from the reading lamp which had been so marvellous a Christmas present three—or was it four—years ago. "I hate you so very much that I can't go on living here. I have gone to stay with Sharon." After which she straightened the bed, drawing the pretty candlewick coverlet over it, and pinned the note with a safety pin in the very middle of it, where it could not fail to be instantly seen.

Then, cautiously and quietly, rattling the metal hangers as little as possible, she reached into the back of the wardrobe for the never-worn, crisply new smocks that were hanging there.

Even with the chair cushion stuffed into the front of her knickers, the effect was still a bit skimpy, unworthy of these billowing folds of material that gleamed darkly in the lamplight. Not until she had wrapped a bath towel round and around her waist as well, securing it with safety pins in four places, was she satisfied with the effect achieved.

And so marvellous was it, so exactly tailored to the dreams of these past weeks, that despite herself the tears dried upon her cheeks, and she stared at herself in the dim reaches of the mirror with a sort of incredulous joy. All a pretence, of course—was she not at this very moment re-deploying the bath towel to better advantage with a new adjustment of the safety pins?—but—ye gods and goddesses—*what* a pretence! What balm it brought, albeit temporarily, to her bruised and battered soul!

And it was not until she was actually on the top deck of the bus, rumbling through the half-darkness of the summer night, that it dawned on her that she couldn't possibly, in this get-up, go and stay at Sharon's.

CHAPTER 8

It was not so much that Sharon's parents would be shocked and incredulous—though of course they would be: it was Sharon herself whom Miranda knew she could not face. Though less well up in the subject than Miranda had succeeded in making herself during the past weeks, Sharon would certainly know enough about the normal course of pregnancy to realise that this sudden and dramatic increase in girth within such a few days could not possibly be genuine. Confronted with the inevitable barrage of searching questions, Miranda would have no alternative but to confess to her friend the silly subterfuge to which she had resorted; and this would lead inevitably to the whole sorry tale of weakness and cowardice in the face of parental pressure, right up to the final ghastly and despicable surrender. Even to a close friend—perhaps particularly to a close friend—the revelation of such shame was unthinkable. Bitterly, Miranda recollected those proud, defiant declarations of hers, in the presence of most of Four A: "They'd have to kill me first!" she'd boasted when Doreen had come out with her tactless suggestion about abortion. She remembered the open-mouthed admiration of her audience, their flattering, half-incredulous awe . . . After all that, to have to go crawling to Sharon, her staunchest supporter, with a miserable confession of humiliation and defeat, knowing, too, that by next term it would be all over the school. Miranda Field isn't pregnant after all. Miranda Field has had an abortion. Miranda Field got cold feet when it came to the crunch, just like we said she would . . .

Unthinkable! Unendurable! She must never see them again, any of them, for as long as she lived! From now on, her existence must be among strangers, people who knew nothing of the girl she had once been, and could pass no judgement on what she had become—had, indeed, not the smallest interest in doing so.

Strangers! How tranquil is their company, how liberating to one whose own self has become a burden beyond enduring! Undemanding, unconcerned, empty of expectations, they take you at face value, looking no further than whatever image you choose, at that moment, to project.

Already, before she had been riding on the bus for as long as five minutes, Miranda was aware of this lightening of burdens; aware, too—intensely and comfortingly aware—of the interest and sympathy her existence was once more arousing. A white-haired old gentleman had already stepped aside to let her go in front, and when she'd boarded the bus the conductress had said "Careful, dear!" putting a hand solicitously under her elbow as she climbed on.

She was special again. Glances of interest and sympathetic speculation were coming her way again, and the comfort of it was beyond belief.

Spurious comfort, obviously. The whole thing was a pretence, nothing more than a silly daredevil charade, she kept dutifully reminding herself; but it was extraordinary, all the same, the way it soothed her wounded spirit and boosted her shattered ego. And indeed, there is no doubt that by projecting with sufficient energy an image in accordance with one's heart's desire, one can indeed infuse that image with a sort of spurious life of its own. Mirrored in the admiring eyes of others, the image acquires a kind of substance, generating feedback which truly feeds, providing genuine scraps of nourishment for such starving, desperate souls as come scavenging in these perilous waste spaces of the mind.

The bus stop at the corner of Sharon's road had long been left behind, but the conductress (no doubt in deference to Miranda's awesome and interesting state) had done nothing about extracting from her any excess fare, and merely asked her if she was sure she was all right . . . was anyone meeting her . . . where would she like to be put down?

"The terminus, please," said Miranda, quite at random, and revelling in every small, unmerited mark of special attention. "Yes, I'll be quite all right, thank you. I live just round the corner from there . . ."

Was there a corner? Would she be caught out, making rash guesses like this out of the blue? For she had no idea at all what terminus they were heading for, or what it was like. It could be a station forecourt, or an amorphous expanse of concrete in the middle of nowhere, not at all the sort of place that anyone could live round the corner from.

But it was all right.

"O.K., love," said the conductress, beginning to lose interest; and presently, with the bus gradually emptying as it neared the end of the route, she settled herself in a front seat, with her back to Miranda, to check her takings. And when the bus finally reached its destination, alongside a triangle of tattered grass overlooked by tall buildings, she was content to call out, "Good night, dear, watch how you go," without looking up.

It was as well, perhaps, that she was thus preoccupied, or her young passenger's behaviour might have roused her suspicions. For Miranda was not behaving in the least like a person who lived "just round the corner," wherever that might be. Instead of walking briskly and purposefully in some definite direction as might be expected of someone nearing home, she stood uncertainly on the grass verge, peering this way and that along the unfamiliar roadway, and clutching her carrier bag of hastily assembled belongings in a state of absolute indecision and completely devoid of plans. She had not the faintest idea of where she was going, or what she meant to do. She didn't even know where she was, except that it was a good hour and a half's bus ride, right across London, from her parents' house.

The lights in the interior of the bus were being extinguished now, and as it pulled away into the darkness, Miranda felt an absurd little pang of homesickness and loss. For it *had* been her home, had it not, for well over an hour: the last home, perhaps, that she would know for many a long day.

"Hi!"

As the small battered Ford drew up beside her, Miranda gave a little start. She wasn't frightened, exactly—like most people who have just suffered a shattering blow, she felt somehow immunised against further disasters—but all the same she stepped back warily as the dim talking outline of a head became visible through the lowered window, and an arm in some sort of a shaggy garment reached out towards the door handle.

"You look like you could use a lift," the pleasant youngish voice was addressing her. "Hop in." He swung the door open invitingly, apparently unaware of, or else unconcerned about, the awful warnings about strange men to which a well-brought-up girl like this one had probably been subjected throughout her formative years.

"Where do you live?" he continued, as Miranda still stood uncertainly at the roadside "—or are you on the way to the hospital?" he amended, after a second look at the bulging, ungainly figure.

Oh dear! Did she really look as pregnant as all *that?* Evidently the bath towel had been overdoing it.

"No . . . Oh no . . . I . . . that is . . ."

"Look, love, you can't hang about here all night, now

can you? The last bus has gone, you know, it's a rotten service these days, they used to run till gone midnight. So come on, there's a good girl, tell me where you want to go and I'll take you"—and then, as she still hesitated, his voice took on a sharper edge: "Hell, I can't just leave you here, now can I? At this time of night, and in your condition—have a bit of sense!" Briefly, his eyes swept her figure once more, and came back to her face.

"You're properly in trouble, aren't you, my dear? Why not tell me all about it while I drive you home? Even though I *am* a Strange Man in a Car, and you don't know me from Adam—"

Had he but known it, he couldn't have hit on a stronger recommendation. She longed, she hungered for people she didn't know from Adam, henceforth they were her blood brothers, her new tribe; from now on she would have dealings only with people she was never going to see again.

"O.K. Thanks," she said, climbing into the car every bit as clumsily as a real pregnant woman, in her anxiety lest the cushion should slip, or the bath towel work itself loose.

"Which way?" he asked, leaning over to lock the door on her side, and then turning on the engine.

What *could* she say? I'm sorry, I haven't decided yet. I'm sorry, I'm afraid I don't live anywhere . . .

It sounded crazy; and while she hesitated, eyes averted, she was conscious of him turning sideways in the driving seat and looking full at her, puzzled and concerned.

She *must* think of something! She *must!* He was being so kind.

"They've turned me out," she improvised at last, wildly. "I've nowhere to go. I can't go home any more."

"Turned you *out!*" He was shocked rigid. "Turned you *out*—a kid like you . . . and in your state! I can't believe it!"

"They're so very respectable, you see," she babbled on, "so very respectable and proper . . ."

The lies flowed easily, almost pleasantly; and presently she found herself weaving threads of truth into the fabric of her fiction.

"They wanted me to have an abortion at the beginning," she told him, "and I wouldn't! . . . I just *wouldn't!*"

Phoney though it all was, a spark of the old pride seemed to stir in her once more, and she raised her head defiantly, her eyes shining in the flicker of oncoming headlights through the windscreen. "I just *would not!*" she repeated, and even as she pronounced the lie, it seemed, somehow, like a sort of truth: a truth about her *real* self, not about the battered, craven thing to which they had reduced her.

"And now," she continued, warming to the story, "now that it's too late for an abortion, they're insisting that I have it adopted—they can insist, you know, legally they can, because I'm under-age. But I won't! I've told them I won't! I'll die sooner . . . !"—even though she knew it was all lies, Miranda felt the wonderful glow of defiance permeating her whole being—". . . and so there was this awful row . . . I kept saying I wouldn't, I absolutely wouldn't, and so in the end they said, well, then, I'd made my bed and I must lie on it, I needn't bother to come home any more . . ."

Had she gone too far? Was it beginning to sound totally implausible and far-fetched? She fell silent, hardly daring to look up at her companion lest she should see a flicker of dawning suspicion on his face; but when at last she did venture to meet his gaze, she saw that his eyes were shining with admiration.

"Christ, but you're a plucky kid!" he exclaimed. "I've never heard anything like it. Every other girl I've ever known would have chickened-out right from the word go —and without any parental pressuring, either. You know what?—it does something for me, it really does, to have run into a bit of pure, undiluted courage for once! It restores my faith in degenerate humanity. And you no more than a kid, too—how old are you?"

"Fifteen," half-whispered Miranda, almost bursting with pride. Such an outburst of unqualified admiration from this attractive young man several years older than herself was intoxicating; and as he put the car into gear and began to pull out into the road, she felt her heart pounding with excitement and quite unwarranted joy.

"Look. I'll tell you what—" evidently he had been thinking hard during the small silence that had supervened while he manoeuvred his way out into the stream of traffic—"why don't I take you back with me to the ancestral home? Alias the Squat? I'm sure we can fix you up with a bed. For tonight, anyway; there's almost always *somebody* gone missing on any given night . . . No, don't be silly, of course it won't be any bother, the girls'll be thrilled."

CHAPTER 9

The girls had indeed seemed thrilled. Now, nearly three weeks later, making her reluctant way through the harsh August sunshine towards the easy-going, slapdash establishment which had become her home, Miranda recalled that first night, the night of her arrival, with poignant clarity, as if looking back on an age of lost innocence. Every detail of that generous, open-hearted welcome from the household of total strangers was branded on her soul for ever. It was past midnight when Tim (for that, she learned, was the name of her rescuer) ushered her through the warped and peeling outside door, and although some of the inhabitants had clearly been roused from their beds by his unceremonious introduction of her into their midst, there was no sign of resentment on any of the sleepy young faces, only eager curiosity and unstinted sympathy and goodwill.

"Preggers! Well, what do you know?" exclaimed the fair, blue-eyed one with freckles, whose name was Alison; while Iris—a few years older than the rest, maybe turned thirty—pushed the swathes of heavy black hair from her eyes, and looked Miranda up and down consideringly before capping Alison's admiring comment.

"Twins, is it?" she drawled, with a humorous lift of the eyebrows, "or triplets?"—and everybody laughed, and was at ease—even Merve, the pink-faced youth who had so far been keeping just a little aloof—not unsympathetic, but just a bit embarrassed, being only nineteen years old and having come straight from a sheltered life with his parents in Sheffield to the even more (in some ways) sheltered life of the Squat here in London. Share and share alike was the motto here, those who happened to have jobs at any particular time supporting those who happened not to; a simple and equitable system to which Merve had always adhered, and to which, ever since he'd left school, he'd been trying to convert his bank manager father, though with singularly little success: which was why, in the end, he'd been driven to leave home.

"She can have Christine's bed, can't she?" someone was saying; and after a brief little interchange about whether the missing Christine might even yet (by now it was past one) put in an appearance, it was decided unanimously to chance it.

And so Christine's bed it was—unmade, devoid of pillowcases, and strewn with miscellaneous items of Christine's underwear; but willing hands soon straightened it, and willing feet kicked the remarkable assemblage of Christine's sandals and odd boots back under the bed where they belonged. Someone brought a hot water bottle, another proffered a hot drink, while the little sallow one called Belinda produced from somewhere a voluminous, comfortably shabby dressing gown. Miranda fell asleep that night feeling cherished and content, as well as mysteriously and profoundly pregnant all over again.

It was Alison who brought her breakfast in the morning—a huge mug of nearly black coffee and a soup plate of cereal swimming in Long Life milk; and while Miranda worked through this repast, Alison sat on the end of the bed in a torn Chinese kimono, and proceeded to "fill her in" about the Squat and its inhabitants.

She, Alison, had been living here for nearly a year now, and described the experience as "mind-blowing" (using the term in its complimentary sense, presumably, since she was smiling reminiscently as she spoke). Like Miranda, she'd arrived unheralded, and well after midnight (apparently this was the accepted mode of taking up residence in this household) and like Miranda, too, she'd been on the run from parental oppression. Here, though, the resemblance ceased; for in Alison's case the pressures had concerned not the ending of a pregnancy, but the continuing of a secretarial course; the main issue being further exacerbated by a number of subsidiary impositions concerning the tidying of her bedroom, the borrowing of the family car, and being expected to get up even on Sundays.

After this, it was Miranda's turn; and naturally—well, what else could she do?—she retailed to Alison the same story as she'd concocted for Tim's benefit last night, and with similarly gratifying results in terms of sympathy and outraged partisanship.

"But that's *awful!* Your own parents—to do a thing like that! It's just monstrous! Gosh, though, you're brave," she added, "I'm sure I'd never have had the nerve to stick it out like that, without any support from *anybody!* I think it's terrific, I really do. I bet Tim was impressed, wasn't he? It's just his kind of thing, the heroic-last-stand bit, boys on burning decks, and all that . . . he's quite a romantic, you know, under all that breezy cynicism. That's how it all got loused up between him and Iris; the dragon-slaying streak in him brings out the Women's Lib in her like bringing a person out in spots. Though actually, when it came to the point . . ."

The sound of hurrying footsteps in the passage outside brought Alison's confidences to an abrupt halt. Her round freckled face swivelled anxiously towards the door, and not until the footsteps had passed on, and the outside door had slammed, did she once more relax.

"I don't know if I should be telling you all this really," she resumed, in a lower voice, "Iris is funny, sometimes, about her private affairs—which it's absolutely, no good being in this place, let me warn you. Still, if you're going to live here, you're going to need all the gen. you can get, especially about Iris, because she's sort of the boss-lady—

insofar as we go in for that sort of thing, which of course we don't, but you know how it is . . ."

"So anyway, the point is, this was her flat originally—Iris's—and when the Council started to requisition houses all along the street—they wanted to pull them down, you see, and put up high-rise blocks, or something, I don't know exactly, it was before my time—anyway, there were a whole lot of protest marches and things—you know, Environment and all that. And that's where Tim came in. He was into the campaign in a big way, a lot of the medical students were, and the nurses, too, because it was going to affect the hospital's catchment area, or something. He was on the committee which advised Iris to sit tight; and it was his idea that she should bring the Squatters in. There's nothing much the Council can do then, you see—I'm not sure why, but Tim had it all worked out. He moved in himself straight away, he was the first Squatter, so's he could help Iris stand up to the Council . . . and actually, in the end, they were quite nice about it, they let everybody stay, and they turned the water back on and everything. We pay them rent now—well, most of us do—and it's all sort of legal, in some complicated sort of way.

"Naturally, Iris was pretty grateful—well, she would be, wouldn't she?—and by the time I got here they seemed well and thoroughly paired off together, she and Tim. There was even talk of them getting married at one point—Iris thought she was pregnant, or something—but luckily nothing came of it. Well, I mean, it would have been ridiculous, wouldn't it, with Tim not even qualified yet, and Iris years older than he is? I don't know how she could ever have thought it *would* come to anything. Anyway, by that time it was all breaking up in any case, because it was around then that Tim . . ."

"Don't believe a word of it! It's all lies!" Catching his name as he passed along the passage, Tim had paused to peer inquisitively round the partially open door. Now he began to edge his way in. "If I were you, Miranda," he advised, "I'd begin as you'll assuredly have to go on, and don't believe *anything* that any of them tells you. They don't *mean* to tell lies—well, not exactly—but the trouble with this place is that it suffers from a sort of Collective Unconscious from which everyone—"

Alison sighed.

"He's always like this when anyone new arrives," she explained to Miranda. "I've only to open my mouth and say one single word to them, and he'll . . ."

"It's not the single words, my dear, it's the battalions," Tim retorted. "I've been counting the decibels through the wall, and wondering when I should come to Miranda's rescue. Recollect, Allie dear, that she's not accustomed to your dulcet tones like we are, you'll be giving her labour pains!"

What fun it was here! What easy, happy relationships they all seemed to have with one another! And how ready and willing they seemed to draw her, too, into the charmed circle of teasing and repartee. It was like being captured by the gravitation of the sun, and drawn into orbit around that mighty source of light and life.

"Alison's been telling me about the Squat, and how it started," Miranda told him eagerly. "It's been awfully interesting."

"Didn't I tell you?—If she's managed to make this dump sound interesting, then she *must* be lying." He moved further into the room. "How are you, love? Feeling all right this morning? I just wanted to make sure you're O.K. before I go off."

How kind he was! How kind they all were! In the warm, smudged sunlight that filtered through the grimy little window, he looked, she thought, even handsomer than he had last night.

"I'm fine. Just fine," Miranda assured him truthfully; and was aware of his eyes resting thoughtfully on her as she lay reclining against her somewhat off-white pillows, her knees crooked up to support the plate of half-eaten cereal.

Had he noticed anything? Was this flat stomach of hers, devoid of its daytime padding, somehow visible to him even beneath this mound of bedclothes?

Impossible!—but all the same, she found herself clutching uneasily at the concealing blankets, bunching them up yet higher against her body. She could not meet his eyes; her heart was thudding wildly; and now—horror of horrors!—she could feel the beginnings of a blush creeping slowly up her neck and towards her cheeks.

But he seemed to suspect nothing. Although his scrutiny was a searching one, it soon became clear that it was simply concern for her welfare, and not any doubts as to her bona fides, which had prompted it. Once reassured, he continued chatting to her, easily and pleasantly, for a few more minutes; and at the end, glancing at his watch, remarked apologetically that he "must be getting home."

"Home?" Miranda was surprised. "But I thought you lived here?"

"I do. That is, I don't. He gave a short laugh. "I live in at the hospital, actually, except that I'm never in—not in my room, that is—and you certainly can't call it living! So —well, I suppose *yes,* I *do* still live here. Sort of. You could say so . . . For the time being . . ."

Here, he dropped his voice, and glanced sharply at the half-open door, as if he had caught some slight but significant sound out there in the passage.

Only for a moment, though; he recovered himself almost immediately, and when he turned again to Miranda, his voice was relaxed and friendly as ever, though still with that note of concern.

"You're sure you'll be all right, then?" he asked, for the second time. "I don't really like leaving you on your own like this, so near your time. When, actually, *are* you expecting it, as a matter of interest?—The actual date?"

The actual date. Oh dear! A direct and specific question like this was more than she'd bargained for. The whole thing really was becoming more than she'd bargained for. Last night, she'd come among them as a stranger among strangers: anonymous, free of identity, untrammelled by past or future: and already this morning they were strangers no more. Already they were her friends, her flatmates, with a right to be concerned about her, to involve themselves in her problems. This principle of Share and Share Alike didn't apply just to money and groceries, but to everything. This non-existent baby of hers already belonged to all of them.

And now, here was Alison, as well as Tim, leaning forward eagerly, eyes fixed on her face, all agog for her answer. She'd got to tell them *something*. And fast.

The actual date . . . the actual date. Oh, not for ages yet, she'd have liked to reply nonchalantly; but how could she, when they all seemed so sure, from her appearance, that the birth was imminent? "Twins is it, or triplets?—" Iris had asked, with raised eyebrows, implying that Miranda was already over-large, even if she was presumed to be at full term. And Tim, too, just glancing at her by the darkened roadside, through the glass of the car window, had at once jumped to the conclusion that she might be on her way to the hospital. In the face of all these expectations—and knowledgeable ones, too—how could she dare put the date more than a very few days ahead?

"August the eleventh," she blurted out, "another five days yet."

Five days. With her own lips, she realised, she had pronounced her sentence of exile from this friendly, infinitely supportive place. After August 11, she must be gone.

"August the eleventh," Tim was repeating thoughtfully. "Well—I suppose that gives us a bit of a margin . . . though of course you can never tell. A few days this way or that. Still . . ."

Taking an old envelope from his pocket, he proceeded

to scribble down for her the various telephone numbers by which she would be able to get him at various hours of the day. Outpatients from 9:30 to 11. Anatomy Room from 11 to 12:30. Junior Refectory 12:45 to 1:30—and so on through the day.

"Be sure and ring me if anything seems to be starting, won't you, love?" he urged her. "Though I'm afraid you'll have to go out to the phone box: a telephone is one of the rich variety of things we haven't got. It's not far, though. If you turn left as you go out of the front door, and up the hill past the church, you'll—No, wait! I've a better idea. Don't try to call me yourself, get Merve to do it. If he's still in bed, then drag him out, or empty a jug of cold water over him, or something. I don't see why he shouldn't do something to earn his keep now and again, the great slob!"

Harsh words, but spoken in the friendliest manner possible; it was clear that Merve, too, was part of the charmed circle, shortcomings and all. Here, in this benign and all-accepting place, people's failings were not merely tolerated, but woven into the very structure of the shared life, one more thread in the bright pattern.

What a lovely way to live!

CHAPTER 10

It all seemed so simple that first morning. After all, she would only be staying here for five days—she had set the deadline herself—and after that they would never see her again. A deception practised on people who are never going to see you again hardly seems like a deception at all. "I wonder what happened to that girl who was going to have a baby?" was the most her rescuers would now and again remark, with decreasing interest, as the weeks went by. Soon, the whole brief episode would have faded from their memories, or be recalled merely as just one more of those bizarre happenings which tend constantly to beat a path to this sort of ever-open door.

That there might, when the time came, be any difficulty about thus vanishing from their lives had not as yet crossed Miranda's mind: and why should it? Had not her predecessor, Christine (whoever she was), vanished in just this fashion, without effort and without fuss? The girl had simply failed to return one night, had never been seen since, and no one (so it seemed) was batting an eyelid. Thus, then, would Miranda do likewise, when the time came. She would walk out of the flat one day, without a word, and never return. They wouldn't try—why should they?—to trace her. For one thing, they couldn't: she hadn't even told them her surname, and—Christian names being the rule in this establishment—they hadn't asked. And for another, it would surely be against their free-and-easy, live-and-let-live principles to mount any kind of a search? Applauding her inalienable right to do her own thing, to run her own life as she pleased, without interference, they'd surely do absolutely nothing? She'd disappear, never be seen again, and their carefree lives would surge onward without her.

Just as had happened with Christine.

Five days, though. Would it be easy to keep up the deception even that long? She yearned, in her heart, to stay and stay and stay in this warm, easygoing place, where she felt so comfortable, so admired, and so safe. But in her head, there was an uneasy niggle of doubt. Was she, in fact, not safe at all, but on the contrary in terrible danger; a danger of discovery that increased inexorably with every extra day, every extra hour, that she remained? It was all right so far, no one suspected a thing, she'd got away with it completely: but five whole days?—wasn't that rather pushing her luck?

Not really. Because luck seemed to be the one thing that was on her side, at the moment. For was it not sheer luck, and nothing else, that had decreed that it should be this Christine, rather than any of the rest of them, who should have chanced to go missing at just this juncture? Because it so happened that Christine's was the only single room in the establishment—and reliably so, since there was no way a second bed could have been squeezed within these narrow walls—if it could, it would have been. It was a poky little room, narrow and cupboard-like, and rather dark, too, since the only illumination came through a grimy little window high up in the wall—but nevertheless, it suited Miranda down to the ground. Here, in privacy, she could don her false pregnancy in the morning and discard it at night without fear of discovery—without *much* fear, anyway. Naturally, in so casual and slaphappy a household as this one, there was always the offchance of someone or another barging into the room uninvited—like the rightful owner, for example, but so far it hadn't happened; and so after a bit there began to seem no point in worrying about it.

Looking back, now, in shame and misery, dragging herself numb with dread through the sullen August heat, Miranda could feel only a sort of dazed incredulity at how little she had worried during those first two or three days; how sure she'd been that the choice was entirely hers, to stay or to go, exactly when she judged fit. She'd felt so happy, somehow, indeed so very nearly pregnant most of the time, that quite often it hardly seemed like a pretence at all. Partly, this was due to the constant reinforcements of the fantasy by her unsuspecting companions. Surrounded by their interest, their concern, and their growing excitement about the coming baby, it was almost impossible not to feel, for quite long stretches of time, that it was all real. When Alison came in one evening with a parcel of pale pink baby wool and a pattern for a matinee jacket, Miranda felt not only touched and grateful, but really excited, and found herself joining eagerly in the ensuing discussion about whether it would be the right size, or should Alison make it a bit bigger by using a larger size of needles than recommended?

"Yes—well—they do seem to think it's going to be quite a big baby," Miranda admitted modestly, and without, at that moment, any sensation of telling a lie. "At my last check-up they said it would be well over eight pounds, more like eight and a half, they thought."

From all of which Alison reasonably inferred that number nine needles would, after all, be the most appropriate, and she settled herself comfortably on the window seat, under the big sash windows wide open to the warm summer air, and set herself to cast on the requisite seventy-two stitches, counting under her breath as she went.

This was the best part of the day, Miranda felt, this hour beween six and seven, when those who had been out at work were beginning to return, flopping down one by one on floor, settee, or window seat, in a mood for relaxation and chatter before the question of whose turn it was to cook dinner began to gather momentum, and before a flurry of preparations closed in upon those who had dates—or hoped that they had—for the coming evening. At this halcyon hour, even those who had done nothing all day—like Miranda and Merve—found themselves partaking with the others in this pleasant (though in their case undeserved) sense of well-earned leisure.

Not that Merve would have agreed that in his case it was undeserved; still less that he had been doing nothing all day, though that was what it looked like to the untutored eye. Merve was writing a novel—a real humdinger of a novel, he assured Miranda—all about a young man of nineteen who had been brought up in Sheffield by blinkered, middle-class parents who had sent him to a school where all the boys who weren't blinkered and middle-class were noisy and rough. Schooldays (seven chapters in all) were followed by an amorphous period dominated by mounting parental obsessions about what our hero (whose name is Henry) is going to *do;* until at last he can stand no more. He kicks over the traces, chucks up his membership of the Young Ramblers' Association, and rushes up to London, where . . .

This was the point the novel had reached when Miranda came on the scene, and this was where, three days later, it was still stuck. Writers' Block was the name given by Merve to his unfortunate condition, and it aroused in his flatmates just the same kind of eager solicitude (pink knitting excepted) as did Miranda's pregnancy. Sympathy, advice, and suggestions for furthering the plot were forthcoming in almost embarrassing profusion, while Merve leaned wearily against the door jamb, limp with the day's non-achievement, and deeply wary—as of course a writer needs to be—of any idea which he hadn't already thought of himself.

How about Henry visits a brothel, suggested one?—but Merve didn't think he knew enough about brothels to make the background convincing. Well, then, have him fall into the clutches of a beautiful spy, someone else proposed: but apparently he hadn't researched this one in sufficient depth either. Well, drugs, then. Get him caught up with a drug ring. Or introduced into a world-famous pop group? . . . What, apart from lying in bed till midday, *does* happen to innocent young men on the loose for the first time in the big wicked city?

Here Miranda put forward a suggestion, diffidently, as became a newcomer: How would it be, she ventured, if he didn't have to be called *Henry?* I mean, with a name like that . . . ?

But *no!* On no account! What an idea! Merve was quite vehement about it, and Miranda, suitably chastened, hastily withdrew from the debate and refrained from making any more suggestions.

Though she could have done, of course. Like, in this Squat where Henry hangs out, there's this bird, see, who's kidding them all she's pregnant when she isn't. Properly pulled the wool over their eyes, she has, thinks she's got away with it; until one evening, summer time it is, and they're all gathered together in the big living room, chatting of this and that, and suddenly she becomes aware of Henry's eyes fixed on her strangely . . .

Miranda felt the red blood rushing to her face, and she hung her head to hide her blazing cheeks.

It was absurd, though! It was ridiculous! Merve wasn't even looking at her at all, let alone strangely! He was staring into space, lost in glum contemplation of the uselessness and futility of all human advice: and as to the others, they too had their attention focussed on something other than her, and had noticed neither the rising nor the fading of her telltale blush. Alison was concentrating on those first vital rows of her knitting, making sure that she was getting the tension right; Iris had already left the room some minutes earlier—it was her turn to cook tonight—and could be heard clattering efficiently in the small kitchen; while Belinda, sitting cross-legged on the floor in her washed-out corduroy slacks, was idly leafing through a magazine.

"I'll read you Caroline's horoscope, shall I?" she said to Miranda, without looking up. "She'll be a Leo, of course—August the eleventh. Which wouldn't be too good, Miranda, since you're a Leo too . . ." (No sooner had Belinda learned the date of Miranda's recent birthday than she'd squealed out in triumph, "There, I *knew* you were a Leo as soon as I saw you! I can always tell!") ". . . But since you're almost right on the cusp, whereas Caroline'll be more towards Virgo, it shouldn't be all that incompatible. Besides, Mars will still be in the ascendant on August eleventh, and—listen!—Venus will be just entering the Third House! That's *very* good, especially for a girl, because . . ."

Miranda wasn't listening, exactly; more lapping it up, like a contented kitten. With Alison on one side fervently knitting up pink wool on her behalf, and Belinda on the other adapting the very stars in their courses to the best advantage of Miranda's baby—how could she feel otherwise than cherished, and content, and utterly secure?

There was no doubt in any of their minds that the baby would be a girl; and it wasn't just on Miranda's say-so, either. Belinda had proved it. Only last night she had applied to Miranda's bulging stomach the String and Ring test, dangling over it someone or other's wedding ring on a length of black cotton. The others had watched, tense and expectant, until at last, impelled by supernatural forces—well, what else, since Belinda swore she was keeping her poised hand *absolutely* motionless?—the ring had begun, slowly at first, and then faster, and more decisively, to move round and round, in an ever-widening circle, under their very eyes.

A girl, this meant. Backwards and forwards, like a pendulum, would have indicated a boy. Belinda was exultant.

"It always works," she declared triumphantly, "for me,

anyway! I've done it on loads of people, and I've never been wrong. Never once! I'm psychic, you see," she explained complacently; and for just one second, Miranda felt her heart stand still.

But it was all right. Psychic or not, Belinda's powers were clearly inadequate to penetrate the appalling secret that lay only inches beneath the twinkling little band of gold that revolved so obediently in miniature orbit, like a phoney little planet round a non-existent sun.

A *girl!* Oh, congratulations, Miranda! That's what you always wanted, isn't it! Half-credulous, and more than half committed to the mighty and unexplored efficacy of sheer wishful-thinking, the girls threw themselves wholeheartedly into plans for the little female child who was to come among them. Pink cot blankets. The dainty, frilled crib that had belonged to someone's sister. Toys, tiny garments, even a cot mattress fell around Miranda like confetti. No, more like warm, life-giving rain, soaking right down into starved and barren soil.

The five days were nearly up now; but how could she leave them as she had planned, without even a word of farewell? How could she throw all this love and kindness back into their faces, like a wet fish, and walk out without a word of explanation, without any exchange of civilities, or arrangements for future meetings? It hadn't been like this even with Christine—this had been her miscalculation right from the very beginning.

An understandable miscalculation, admittedly. From their casual and cavalier manner of re-allotting the absent girl's bed to a total stranger, without so much as a by-your-leave, Miranda had got the impression that this must be the house style: just part of the non-interfering, do-your-own-thing philosophy on which this establishment claimed to be based. Out of sight, out of mind: if someone disappeared, then that was her right and her privilege; you just wrote her off, replaced her with whoever happened to turn up, and carried on without a backward look. And so thus (Miranda reasoned) it would be with her likewise, when her turn came to disappear.

How wrong she'd been in at least some of these assumptions became abundantly clear to her within her first forty-eight hours. Scrupulously though they might concede to the vanished Christine her inalienable right to do her own thing, they clung with equal pertinacity to their own inalienable right to chatter and gossip about this thing to their hearts' content, analysing and dissecting it down to its last luscious details. They all knew by now exactly where Christine must have gone, and why; and when they weren't talking about Miranda's baby during the long summer twilights, sprawling around among the shabby armchairs and frayed cushions of the big, cluttered room, they were talking about Christine's love life, and where (which would seem to be almost everywhere) she'd gone wrong.

"How she can go crawling back to Keith after all that business with Topsy, I'll never understand," Iris remarked, surveying the polished ovals of her nails through narrowed lids. "And as for giving in like that about the bathroom curtains!"—here she shrugged scornfully—"she must be out of her tiny mind!"

"Oh, I don't know." Alison's fingers were flashing through and around the pink wool for Miranda's non-existent baby, and her face glowed, madonna-like, in the last of the sunset. "After all, Iris, she does really love him. Well, she must, mustn't she?—look at that time on the Underground . . . !"

They all laughed uproariously with delighted reminiscence. Clearly, whatever had happened between this Keith and this Christine on the Underground had been rich enough, and bizarre enough, to have become a household joke, a delightful in-group reference, welding them together in shared merriment.

For the newcomer, though, these sorts of exchanges

were most tantalising. You couldn't keep *on* saying, who's Topsy, and *which* time on the Underground, and where do the bathroom curtains come in?—it would be just too tedious for the rest of them. Oh, well; that's the way it was, being a new girl. Miranda would just have to sit quietly, listening, picking up what she could, and piecing it together, until gradually, as the days went by, it would all become clear to her, and she, too, would be sharing in the gossip and the laughter . . .

As the days went by . . . But for her, Miranda, the days *weren't* going to go by, not more than one or two of them, anyway. By tomorrow, or the day after at latest, she must be gone.

And when it was all over, when Alison's knitting needles clicked no longer; when Belinda's fairy-godmother predictions ceased, and the girls chattered about her no more, then Baby Caroline would be gone, too. Gone in some final, irrevocable way which despite the abortion, despite everything, had somehow, as yet, not quite happened.

"Coffee, anyone?" Belinda was on her feet, numbering off the assembled company without reference to the replies—it wasn't as if anyone ever did say "no" to this sort of offer.

"Black for you, Iris?" she opined; "and you too, Merve, if you're really going to be rewriting that chapter all night. Milk-and-a-dash for you, Miranda, it's better for the baby; remember what Tim said about too much caffeine . . . No, no love, you stay where you are, I'll do it. Why don't you put your feet up?—move over, Merve, and let Miranda have the whole of the settee. She's the one who's pregnant, not you . . . Yes, I *know* that writing a novel is as painful as giving birth, you've told us about ten million times, but all the same, it can't give you varicose veins, now can it!"

"*I* haven't got varicose veins, either," Miranda was beginning, with a little laugh; but Iris interrupted her:

"Funny you're having so little trouble with your legs, isn't it?" she remarked pleasantly. "No cramps. No swollen ankles. Nothing. My sister had all sorts of aches and discomforts in the last month—although she never got to half your size! You've been awfully lucky, haven't you?"

Was Miranda imagining it, or was there in the older girl's pleasant, conversational tone a hint of something other than ordinary, kindly interest? This was not the first time that Iris had called attention in a perfectly bland and casual sort of way to some feature of Miranda's condition which struck her—so she claimed—as being just slightly different from the norm. She couldn't, like Tim, lay claim to any specialised medical training in the field, but she did seem to possess an unconscionable number of sisters, cousins, and girlfriends, whose pregnancies had every one of them differed in some small but disconcerting way from Miranda's.

"You're carrying very high, aren't you, Miranda?" she'd remarked only yesterday, eyeing Miranda up and down as she stood at the cooker, stirring the big pan of soup thereon. "Usually, it tends to drop during the last month, and you go quite a noticeably different shape. The head *is* engaged, isn't it? It should be, by now."

Up to a point, Miranda was well able to counter expertise with expertise, so thoroughly had she read up the subject during recent weeks. But this was a new one to her.

"Oh yes. Oh, I think it is," she answered hastily; and at that very moment Tim walked into the kitchen. By some unfortunate chance it always seemed to happen that, despite his long hours at the hospital, Tim invariably chanced to be around, and within hearing, just when Iris was making her casual but disconcerting observations.

"What's this about the head not being properly engaged?" he asked sharply, looking from Miranda to Iris, and then back to Miranda again. "Was that what they said, at your last check-up?"—and then, with a sudden sharpening of anxiety: "You *are* going to your check-ups still, aren't you Miranda? I know you told us the hospital you're booked into is miles away, but all the same—listen, I'll tell you what! I'll drive you there. Just let me know when your next appointment is, and I'll get the time off somehow . . . you shouldn't be travelling that sort of distance on public transport at this stage. Besides, I'd like to have a word with your doctor . . . there's just one or two things I'm not quite happy about . . . Oh, now, sweetie, there's no need to look so horrified! I don't mean there's anything wrong with the baby, I'm sure it's fine, absolutely fine! It's just—well—with your parents out of the picture like this, and you so determined to keep it that way—well, *someone's* got to see that you're being properly looked after. Surely you can see that?

"So go look at your appointment card, there's a good kid, and we'll fix it right now. The only time I absolutely *can't* do is Thursday afternoon, between two and four . . ."

CHAPTER 11

And thus it came about that it was on Thursday afternoons, between two and four, that a certain non-existent Dr. Fergusson held his mythical ante-natal clinic at a St. Benedict's Hospital of infinitely indeterminate location. Though Miranda's first visit to this establishment was exhausting in many ways, and involved sheltering for two hours in a station waiting room as well as mooching round and round unfamiliar streets until the requisite number of hours had been filled, she nevertheless managed to arrive back at the flat in good spirits, and full of the news that this Dr. Fergusson had pronounced her to be perfectly O.K.

Rejoicings all round. Anxiety levels down to zero. Life resumed its happy-go-lucky routine until, almost before she knew it, *next* Thursday was upon her, and off Miranda had to go again, reluctantly this time, and with glum anticipation of the long, tedious hours ahead. Five of them at least would have to be whiled away, for so remote had she made St. Benedict's sound—to explain why nobody had ever heard of it—that she could not also claim that it could be reached by public transport in anything less than one and a half hours, at the very least. So three hours' travelling had to be presumed, on top of the two hours spent hanging about among all those non-existent maternity cases with their non-existent symptoms, ranging from disembodied blood pressure to spectral haemorrhoids. Last time, Miranda had fallen down a bit on these sorts of details, and Iris had expressed mild surprise that she knew so little about her fellow patients, even after all these months of attending ante-natal clinic together. And so this time, Miranda was determined to make good the deficiency, and spent most of her five hours in the public library looking up Obstetrics and Home Midwifery, to such good effect that even Iris could not fault her. As she talked, she even began to feel herself that all these detailed anecdotes of her afternoon at the clinic must, in some sense, be true; including Dr. Fergusson's reiterated assurances that she was getting on fine, nothing to worry about at all; and the baby likewise. And it did seem perfectly plausible: in this non-existent world of non-existent mothers and visionary symptoms, the non-existent Baby Caroline fitted in like a dream.

All the same, her report on this occasion, detailed and reassuring though it was, did not quite allay her friends' anxiety as her last week's account had done. She was now (by her own calculation) more than a week overdue, and though they were very kind, and very, very reassuring, she could feel, this time, a build-up of anxiety, and indeed of puzzlement, which nothing could stem. When Thursday came round for the third time, and she set off yet again on her futile and increasingly implausible errand, she knew, with secret inner panic, that it was for the last time. She could not keep it up much longer. Before next Thursday came, *something* would have had to happen. What, exactly, it would be, she did not even dare to wonder.

Meantime, there was today to be got through. Five hours, to be filled up somehow, somewhere.

In the park, it was too hot. In the library, it was too boring. She'd gone in there with the intention of relaxing in the quiet and the coolness, whiling away the long afternoon by reading the papers, or maybe browsing along the shelves until she came across something amusing enough, or gripping enough, to distract her mind from its pre-occupations, ever more insistent as day followed day.

But it was no use. She could concentrate on nothing. Sitting at one of the empty, polished tables in the quiet room, her book unread in front of her, all she could do was think, think, think. The same old thoughts, over and over again, without respite, and leading nowhere. By now, her brain was like a gramophone record, going round and round, senselessly, in the same old grooves, until suddenly it screeched to a halt, in the exact same place, time after time: the place from which there was no further to go. Then, back to the beginning again—on . . . and on . . . and on . . .

Already, the baby was more than two weeks overdue; her friends at the Squat were growing more and more bothered about her day by day, more and more concerned and puzzled. Tim, in particular, armed with professional knowledge which was proving impossible to laugh off, was becoming more and more insistent; only last night, he'd been on at her in a big way. What were they *doing* about her at that damn hospital, he'd demanded, quite angrily. Hadn't they said anything about an induction? Or having her in for observation? What the hell did they think they were playing at? And don't give him that one about having "got her dates wrong"—hadn't they told her almost three weeks ago that the baby was even then eight pounds or over? How *could* they let it drag on like this, without so much as taking her in for a proper investigation?—and who *was* this damn doctor, anyway? Was he a qualified obstetrician? For two pins, Tim would ring him up himself, medical etiquette or no medical etiquette . . .

Two pins. That's not much of a bulwark to stand between yourself and total, irretrievable disaster. If Tim *did* ring up this non-existent Dr. Fergusson (and who knew that there might not be such a person?) in this non-existent hospital, and started cross-questioning him about his non-existent patient . . . At this point, Miranda's imagination stopped dead, refusing, like a recalcitrant horse, to take so impossible a fence. It baulked, veered sideways, reared, and refused again. Any direction—any direction at all—except this one.

So suppose she simply disappeared, as she'd originally planned? Disappeared; vanished from their lives forever, without a word of explanation? Apart from the monstrous ingratitude of such a course, there was no chance, any longer, that it would work.

"I'd ring them up myself," Tim had threatened, worried and frowning; and if this was the way he felt about the mere non-arrival of the baby, then how was he going to react if Miranda herself (still, as he would suppose, in this precariously overdue condition) were simply to vanish?

He'd ring up every hospital in London, that's what he'd do. And as soon as he'd satisfied himself that both Dr. Fergusson and his ante-natal clinics were figments of the imagination, then, inevitably, he would ring the police.

There seemed no chance that Miranda was not, by now, somewhere in the police records as a Missing Person; no chance, either, that it would take them long to match up Tim's description of her with that which her parents must have given many days earlier.

Within twenty-four hours, Tim would know everything. He would know about the abortion: about her craven and despicable surrender to parental pressure. He would remember her empty boasting that first night in the car, her phoney heroics; would remember, too, the way he'd been taken in by it all.

"Christ, but you're a plucky kid!" he'd said—she could still recall the respect, the wonder in his voice—"I've never heard anything like it! Every other girl I've ever known would have chickened-out right from the word go!"

As she, Miranda, had in fact chickened-out; and soon, terribly soon, he was going to know it. Those eyes that in the darkness of the car had been shining with admiration for her courage—what was their expression going to be when he learned the truth about her cowardice and lies? When he learned that his sympathy, his kindness, his professional concern were become a mockery, a laughing stock?

It *mustn't* happen! It *mustn't!* Surely there was *some* way . . . ?

Already it was five o'clock, and the library was beginning, gently but relentlessly, to close, with soft-footed assistants gliding purposefully this way and that, hell bent on the polite and soundless disturbance of everyone. Thrusting her book back on the shelf as randomly as she'd extracted it, Miranda gathered up her sparse belongings and stumbled out into the sunshine.

The glare was terrific after the muted coolness of the reading room; the heat struck at her as if she had stepped through into an oven. She would have liked to go straight home and run a cold bath, but of course this was out of the question. There was still an hour to fill in before she dared reappear at the flat, and face, once again, the thickening miasma of concern and puzzlement, the barrage of kindly, anxious questions.

Could she face them? As she moved, unseeing, through the sweating, swaying crowds Miranda visualized, all over again, how it would be. The anxiety; the forced cheerfulness; the pretence that there was nothing to worry about. The cosseting, too, the cushions and the cups of tea, and the mounting bewilderment.

But didn't the doctor say *anything*, Miranda, dear? Isn't he worried about you by now?—I mean, of course, there's nothing to worry about *really*, heaps of people go overdue, but all the same, Tim did say . . .

Slower grew Miranda's steps, and slower; and the heat beat down relentlessly on her smooth, glowing young skin and her shining hair.

What *could* she do? What *could* she? Even suicide was

no answer, for when they identified her dead body, as of course they would, they would identify her deception with it, as surely as in life. Tim, and all the rest of them, would still learn of her cowardice and her treachery, blazoned, as likely as not, over every newspaper in the land. *Everyone* would know.

No, death was no solution. What was it John Donne had said, in his Defence of Suicide?—"Methinks I have the keys to my prison in mine own hand"—which is well enough, no doubt, if all that is the matter with you is melancholia and debts.

But for Miranda there were no such keys, her prison was co-extensive with the entire reading public—not to mention television viewers as well—and the duration of her sentence was the life span of all who had ever known her, and who would carry to their graves the memory of her lies, her treachery, and her craven, unforgiveable surrender.

What *could* she do? What *could* she?

Slower and slower still. Her feet dragged on the hot pavement, and with every step in the direction of the Squat, her whole body flinched, her stomach churned. The streets were growing familiar now as she approached the environs of her current domicile; and at last, right on the corner of the road, she found herself coming to a halt, stopped in her tracks by a thought so tremendous, a plan so bold, and yet so simple and so obvious, that it was amazing it hadn't occurred to her before.

"I must have the baby tonight," she said to herself; and quietly turned about and walked back the way she had come. Anyone watching would have assumed she'd suddenly remembered some extra item on her shopping list, so abrupt was the change of direction, and so coolly purposeful the expression on the smooth young face, tanned almost golden by the stored-up sun of all these long, dry summer days.

CHAPTER 12

"Baby snatched from pram in busy high street!" screamed the headlines; and although Mrs. Field, in common with almost every other woman in the country, scanned the item with sharp attention, the idea never for one moment crossed her mind that her missing daughter might possibly have had a hand in the affair. Later, there were not a few of her acquaintances to upbraid her with not having been more perspicacious; but then it is easy, is it not, to be wise after the event. And, too, it must be remembered that at this time Norah Field hadn't even realised that her daughter *was* missing—not in any definite, official sense. That the girl was away from home, and that the date of her return had been left vague—this, of course, she knew very well, having herself altruistically been party (or so she thought) to all the arrangements.

That Miranda should go on holiday with Sharon Whittaker and her parents to their Derbyshire cottage had seemed a godsend of an idea, after all the trauma and misery at home. In that lovely countryside, enjoying long healthy walks over the hills in the company of her best friend, and with the sensible Whittaker parents in the background, surely Miranda would recover fast from the shock and disappointment of the abortion. All that irrational rage and resentment would quickly fade away, and she would return from the holiday her own happy, loving self again, all forgotten and forgiven. And even before that, of course, there would be letters. Hardly had the Whittakers set off on their holiday, than Norah Field found herself watching for the post with beating heart. Just a postcard to start with, no doubt; to be followed by a slightly stilted, awkward letter—to which Norah's reply would be so warm, so loving, so overflowing with forgiveness that all the barriers would be down, the air cleared; and thereafter would arrive, by almost every post, the amusing, newsy letters that Miranda had always been accustomed to send when on holiday away from home . . .

But there was nothing so far; and as a week became a fortnight, and still no news, Norah found herself trying to hide the intensity of her disappointment even from herself. Postal delays, perhaps? A strike of some sort, or a go-slow? This would explain, too, why Mrs. Whittaker hadn't written either. It was odd not to have had a single word from her, not even a telephone call to confirm the invitation issued so abruptly by Sharon, on the very eve of their departure. Maybe Mrs. Whittaker was embarrassed, having learned from Sharon of her friend's unfortunate situation, and just couldn't think what to say?

Meantime, Norah didn't even know the address of the Derbyshire cottage, or how long they were all staying there, or anything. There was nothing she could do but wait; and of course it was something, at least, to know that Miranda was safe and well.

Thus loyally, and with consummate cunning, had Sharon succeeded in keeping faith with her vanished friend; and all this without the faintest idea of what was going on, or what the secret could possibly be with which she'd been tacitly, but unmistakably, entrusted.

It was a miracle, really, that she'd even spotted that there *was* a secret. Miranda had told her absolutely nothing, and had it not been for her, Sharon's presence of mind, together with her swift and delicate antennae for parental fuss in any shape or form, the whole thing could have been absolute disaster. For when, at about eleven o'clock on that first night, Mrs. Field had rung up the Whittakers' house and asked to speak to her daughter, Sharon (who had luckily been the one to pick up the phone) had been on the very brink of saying, "I'm sorry, I'm afraid she's not here," when something—some indescribable nuance in Mrs. Field's voice—had warned her that here was Trouble. Trouble with a big "T." What the trouble was she could not tell, for Miranda had told her nothing whatever—indeed, for these last two or three days seemed to have been inexplicably avoiding her old friend—but whatever it was, whatever Miranda might be up to, Sharon's loyalty was unshakeable. If Miranda had told her mother that she was here at Sharon's, then here she should unquestionably be.

"I'm sorry . . ." (she managed to change direction just in time) "I'm sorry, Mrs. Field, she's in the bath at the moment. Is it urgent?"

The suspense was almost unbearable. Suppose Miranda's mother were to say, as she well might, "Well then, would you ask her to give me a ring when she comes out?" *Then* what was Sharon to do?

But it didn't happen. With an almost audible release of breath in sheer thankfulness, Sharon heard the tension and anxiety drain out of Mrs. Field's voice.

"Oh! Oh, well then, *that's* all right! No, don't bother her, dear, it doesn't matter, I just wanted to make sure she'd turned up all right. Just give her my—my love—and tell her I'll ring again in the morning . . ."

In the *morning?* So Miranda must have told her mother that she was *staying* here?

Well, so be it. No doubt all would be made clear before long, and meantime the important thing was that it should be Sharon, and not either of her parents, who reached the telephone should it ring before the two of them left for work in the morning.

It didn't; but it rang almost immediately afterwards—the man about the gutters. He was coming—or maybe *wasn't* coming, Sharon was too flustered to take in minor details—at ten o'clock on Saturday morning; and before Sharon had managed to devise a message for her father sufficiently wide-ranging to embrace both possibilities, the phone went again; and this time, it *was* Mrs. Field.

Miranda couldn't be having *another* bath. Sharon did some quick thinking.

"I'm afraid she's still asleep, Mrs. Field," she declared cheerfully, though with a thudding heart. "You see—" here she forced an apologetic little laugh, "I'm afraid we were playing my tapes until all hours last night . . . she's sleeping like the dead! But I'll wake her, shall I? . . . If it's important?"

Once again, a breath-stopping gamble; but necessary in the interests of an easy, natural atmosphere.

"Oh no! No . . . no . . . don't do that. It's not necessary. No, no, it's nothing, dear . . . not important. Thank you so much. I'll try again later . . ."

Ping! Breath released again. Heart resumes beating again. The gamble has paid off, and all is well. Until next time.

There would *be* a next time; that was for sure. Hell, what *was* Miranda up to? For the first time, Sharon allowed herself some stirrings of resentment. Why couldn't the wretched girl telephone? Or somehow get *some* sort of message through to her, give her at least *some* idea of what was going on; of what was expected of her, and for how long? Being faithful unto death is all very fine and noble, but you do need to know what you are being faithful *about*.

The phone again; and Sharon, trembling, leaped into action.

It was the gutter man again, this time something about Monday afternoon: though whether this was as well as, or instead of, or nothing to do with, the Saturday morning appointment, she was too rattled to take in. Anyway, he either was or wasn't coming, either morning or afternoon, on either Monday or Saturday, or maybe contrariwise, if that was convenient?

"Oh yes, *yes!*" gasped Sharon thankfully; indeed, "convenient" was altogether too feeble a term for the sheer marvellousness of the call not being anything about Miranda. "Oh *yes,* that would be *super!* Oh, *thank you!*"

The gutter man must have been not a little startled. Such overwhelming gratitude and warmth was not the usual response of his customers to delays and cancelled appointments. Still, you never know your luck. It just goes to show.

Twice more the telephone rang through the quiet house—once for the people upstairs, and once about an overdue library book. Perfectly innocuous calls, both of them, but by this time Sharon's nerves were all on edge waiting for the next one, and planning what on earth to say when it came.

In bed still? In the bath? In the loo? Out shopping? There weren't all that many excuses on which to ring the changes . . . Sooner or later Miranda's mother was going to suspect something.

And suspect something she did, as was made clear by her very first words when Sharon next picked up the phone.

"Sharon, dear, please don't lie to me any more," she started off, causing Sharon's heart to hurl itself against her ribs in terror. "I know you mean well, dear, I know you are only doing it to spare my feelings, but please, *please* stop it, and tell me the truth. Miranda's refusing to come to the telephone, isn't she? She doesn't want to speak to her own mother any more. That's it, isn't it? *Isn't* it?"

Well, really, this *was* a way out of it! It really was! Sharon would never have thought of it herself in a hundred years; but having it handed to her on a plate like this . . .

"Look, Mrs. Field, I'm awfully sorry, but . . . well . . . since you've guessed . . . well, yes, I'm afraid it *is* a bit like that, just at the moment . . ."

Well, and it was, too. It must be. Nothing short of a most *frightful* row with her mother would have induced Miranda to take flight in this precipitate and unprecedented manner. Sharon wasn't lying, then, but telling what must be (surely it must?) the sober truth: after a row on that scale, Miranda *wouldn't* be feeling like speaking to her mother.

"Yes, Mrs. Field," she repeated, more firmly. "I'm awfully sorry, but I'm afraid there's no way I can get her to come to the phone . . . not just now, anyway . . ."

And this again was as true a word as she had ever spoken.

CHAPTER 13

"Norah! Norah! Did you listen to the News just now? That baby was snatched from its pram—apparently it all happened quite near here! Not ten minutes away from the bus station!—Just imagine!"

Janine Parkes, a bouncing divorcée in her forties, with lacquered golden curls, beautifully manicured hands, and a pair of tattered down-at-heel slippers quite good enough for popping in on Norah, had burst in from next door; and although it was not yet nine o'clock, was already settling herself cosily at Norah's kitchen table in expectation of a nice cup of coffee. She felt confident of a warm welcome, so bad was the news with which she had come primed.

"They still haven't found it, you know," she reported, leaning forward confidentially, elbows on table. "They've had police dogs out all night . . . and house-to-house enquiries all over the neighbourhood . . . Isn't it *awful!* I don't know how a person can do such a thing . . . And when you think of that poor young mother—well, not all *that* young, actually, not by her looks anyway. She looked really quite middle-aged—and that awful jumper she was wearing—you know, really *frumpy*. They had her picture in the *Gazette* this morning, did you see it, and all those children lined up on either side of her, left to right you know—all their names and ages. Look, here you are—I brought it over to show you."

As a matter of fact, Norah had already seen the picture,

but all the same she took the proferred copy, and while the kettle boiled she had another look.

Janine was absolutely right—though not, of course, particularly kind, in view of the unhappy circumstances. The woman *was* frumpish. There was no other word for it. With her sagging jowls, her layer upon layer of ill-fitting and unseasonable woollies, and her grimly down-turned lips, it was impossible to see her as a figure of tragedy or high drama. The lineaments of that heavy face were less those of grief than of one damn thing after another, with this the final bloody straw. Nor were the pack of children alongside in much better case. They looked awkward rather than grief-stricken, and a bit embarrassed, as if no one had told them how they ought to feel. Well, I suppose no one has, mused Norah. Having a three-week-old baby sister stolen from the family circle isn't a thing that happens all that often; there aren't any rituals for it.

Steam spurted from the kettle, the lid leaped and chattered, and Norah went through the routine of making coffee, though she herself had only just finished breakfast, having made a late start this morning.

Milk? Sugar? Sorry there aren't any biscuits, I had to rather rush through my shopping yesterday. I've been a bit disorganised lately, since—

No, she didn't want to talk about Miranda, not if she could help it. And certainly not to Janine. Fortunately, Janine did not seem to notice the hiatus, she was still busily scanning the paper for further items of information to titillate her sense of outrage.

Outside *Sainsbury's*, would you believe it? She, Janine, shopped there quite often, or would do if it wasn't for the parking . . . and so if this shocking event had only taken place a week . . . a month . . . a year ago, and if instead of being on a Thursday it had been on a Saturday, and if it had been morning instead of late afternoon—why, then she, Janine herself, might actually have been there when it happened!

"Now, that's the thing I really *don't* understand," she remarked, gently censorious as the indubitably non-involved can afford to be, "how all these people—'Hundreds of shoppers' it says—how they can all have just *let it happen!* Now, if *I'd* caught sight of someone stealing a baby . . . !"

They argued, for a few desultory minutes, the justification or otherwise of this reproach. By what signs or symptoms could the ordinary passer-by be expected to recognise such a crime, even if it should take place under his very eyes? Snatching a baby isn't like snatching a handbag: all that the outsider would observe would be a young woman lifting from its pram—tenderly and solicitously, in all probability—a baby that he would take for granted was her own. Well, he *oughtn't* to take it for granted, Janine countered: people should check on these things. What, on *everything?* Every time you see someone opening a car door, it *might* be someone other than the owner, mightn't it? Soon, the streets would be jammed solid with everyone checking on everyone else, and business would come to a standstill.

"You wouldn't talk like that if it was *your* baby that had been stolen!" Janine retaliated, illogically but with crushing effect; almost anyone can be persuaded to agree that two and two make five if the assertion that they make four can be made to seem heartless and lacking in compassion.

Besides, she did have a point, of sorts.

"I'm quite absolutely sure," Janine resumed, "that someone *stealing* a baby from a pram would behave quite absolutely differently from a real mother. There'd be all sorts of signs . . . Here, listen to this—*this* is the kind of thing I mean . . ."

Here she proceeded to read out in full detail an account (which, as it happened, Norah had already read for herself, as well as hearing it on the News) of how some woman had noticed—or claimed she had noticed—a young girl with long fair hair leaning over a pram, whispering to the baby, and crying. Nothing seemed to have come of this clue—there was so far no iota of proof that the pram that was being cried over was the same as that from which a baby was snatched—but no doubt the police were following it up. If there was anything in it, then in due course they'd hear all about it on the News.

A young girl with long fair hair, crying.

Later, Janine was to declare that she'd known all along that it was Miranda Field, from the very first moment she'd read about this fair-haired girl; but you'd never have guessed it at the time. On the contrary, it was at just about this point in the conversation that her interest in the whole matter appeared to flag, as if she felt that the episode had by now been milked dry of all it had to offer of coffee-morning scandal. And when, a little later, she *did* come round to the subject of Miranda, it was in a totally different connection.

Like everyone else in their circle, Janine had heard rumours of Miranda's little slip-up, and she assumed (again like everyone else) that the Fields, enlightened couple that they were, would have arranged an abortion for their daughter. It was unthinkable that they'd have any old-fashioned moral scruples about it—wasn't Edwin Field a prospective left-wing candidate of some sort, and thus wholly in favour of the Permissive Society in all its manifestations?

Probably, the whole thing was over and done with by now; but it was tantalizing—it really was—not to have been told *any* of the details while it was all going on. Such close neighbours, too, she and Norah, and still friends of a sort, despite Norah's reluctance, at the time of Janine's divorce, to corroborate Janine's claim to be a battered wife. True, she hadn't *looked* battered, whereas Charlie had, rather; but surely women should stand together on this sort of issue, otherwise what is Women's

Lib all about? Wife-battering is so heinous a crime that a man shouldn't get away scot free even if he *hasn't* done it.

Still, all this was water under the bridge now, or would be if Charlie would stop being so difficult about the maintenance. One way and another, she and Norah Field had been through a lot together as measured in gallons of tea and coffee over the years. It was mean of Norah, now, to be so secretive over this Miranda business. More than mean, indeed: it was downright anti-social. For is it not very nearly a duty, if something bad happens to you, to feed it into the neighbourhood pool of gossip? To donate it, as it were, to those with less eventful lives than your own? Some people are stingy with their misfortunes as others are stingy over money. Still, this is no reason for letting them get away with it.

"Miranda still on holiday, is she?" Janine asked, carefully casual, and with an air of simply making conversation; but when nothing more revealing than a non-committal murmur of assent was forthcoming, she allowed herself to press a little harder.

"She's been gone for more than a fortnight, hasn't she?" she continued; and when this, too, evoked nothing beyond an affirmative nod, Janine, with a pleasant smile, moved in for the kill.

"It seems funny, not seeing her around all this time. I *quite* thought last night that she must be back . . . all that pop music . . . My goodness, you could hear it three gardens away! I could have *sworn* it came from here . . . one of your upstairs windows . . . But I suppose . . ."

When you leave a sentence unfinished specially to give your companion a chance to interrupt, and then she doesn't, it can be most annoying. Janine gave a little shrug of irritation and impatience. Really, Norah was being impossible! What a waste of a morning! And not even any biscuits, either . . . But before this silent catalogue of her hostess's omissions and shortcomings had got any further, the object of them raised her head and gave an apologetic little laugh.

"Oh, *that!* Yes, I'm afraid it *was* from here, actually—I'm awfully sorry if it disturbed you. Sam's home, you see—" here she paused, as if waiting for the significance of this to sink in; then. "Yes, he's back home again—you know, from that Overland trip to India."

Ah, Sam! The delinquent son; the blot on the Field escutcheon. Janine pricked up her ears.

"And you know what?" Norah was laughing again, wryly. "He's brought back this extraordinary friend with him, that he picked up in Katmandu, or somewhere. A terribly thin, disapproving young man who's allergic to whatever it is our pillows are stuffed with, and goes on and on about us being middle class. He told me last night that the amount of food I'd put on his plate would keep an Indian peasant for a week. I nearly asked him if his second helping would have kept *another* Indian peasant for *another* week, but I didn't dare because Sam thinks he's wonderful. He's into the Wider Consciousness, Sam says, and so we're going to be stuck with him for weeks and weeks while he seeks the Reality within the Reality, which apparently takes ages and ages, and is why his parents won't have him home, they're sick of it. He's recovering from hepatitis, too, so we have to swill out every single cup and glass with boiling water after he's drunk from it—and in secret, too, so as not to hurt his feelings. Sam nearly killed me when he smelt Dettol in the bathroom last night, he accused me of trying to disinfect Yoshi as if he was a *thing,* a non-sterile object . . . Well, he is, isn't he? Hepatitis is no joke, after all. And then of course I've got poor Edwin to worry about as well, you know how he relies on me to keep things from him, and how *can* I when they're *both* of them around the place *all* day long? And then the pop records as well—I *will* do something about that, Janine, I promise I will, but just at the moment, I'm having to be so tactful it's not true! What with telling Edwin that it's only for another day or two, and telling Sam that of course his friends are welcome for as long as they like to stay—Oh, dear, I *never* seem to stop telling lies from morning till night! You know how it is! And now, Janine, if you don't awfully mind, I really think I ought to be . . ."

Reluctantly, Janine took her leave. It was a pity that it should all have to finish now, just when it was getting really interesting; but at least it was good to know that Sam was still being a problem despite his travels. Having heard so little about him all these months, Janine had almost begun to fear that he was going the way so many of her friends' problem children had gone, one after another getting jobs, coming off drugs, going back to finish their degrees—really, it was quite getting her down, especially just now, with her own life going so rottenly.

A blast of discordant noise from the top floor of the Fields's home cheered her a little as she made her way past the side entrance and into her own garden. Soon, the rest of the neighbours would be complaining, and that was always fun. Jauntily, and more or less in time with the screeching music, she almost skipped up the path and into the pleasant, well-appointed home which Charlie was still rabbiting on about his half of; but who cared? Charlie was a born loser—that was the very thing that had wrecked the marriage, actually—and so let him damn well lose this one, too!

It wasn't such a bad old life: and there was still half a bottle of gin left in the dining room cupboard. Not that Janine was letting her troubles turn her into an alcoholic, or anything like it, but it did give you something to look forward to in the mornings when coffee time was over.

As she sipped, it crossed Janine's mind that she hadn't after all succeeded in worming out of her neighbour any of the low-down on Miranda and her misfortunes; the Sam saga had somehow intervened, and all that stuff about the hepatitis and everything. It was odd that Norah was being so uninhibitedly communicative about her problems with her son, and yet so obstinately silent about those of her daughter. Surely she wasn't *ashamed* of Miranda's predicament? Schoolgirl pregnancies were two-a-penny these days, and abortion the obvious and easy answer in any modern, enlightened family of even mildly left-wing leanings . . .

It was this last phrase, drifting through her mind, which brought Janine up with a jerk; it illumined, in a single, blinding flash, the whole tantalizing puzzle.

Of course! Fancy not having thought of it before! It was not their daughter's pregnancy that the Fields were so ashamed of, nor the abortion. No, it was the fact that they must have had the operation done *privately!* To people of their egalitarian convictions, *this* was the disgrace, *this* the unmentionable shame, the skeleton in their left-wing cupboard!

Poor old Norah! What a come down!

Janine smiled pityingly, and treated herself to a second little drink, as if in celebration.

CHAPTER 14

Meanwhile, far away on the other side of London, Merve was staring resentfully into his typewriter, trying to piece together the trampled remnants of dialogue that had been going so marvellously last night before the interruption. He had just got it exactly the way he wanted it, in all its mordant realism, and had been about to immortalise it in a top copy and three carbons, when—wham!—there had imploded into the flat the Great Happening, scattering before it all traces of consecutive thought, and drowning inspiration in squeals of imbecile amazement.

"A *girl!*" they'd shrieked, back and forth through the juddering doorways. "A *girl!* Isn't that *wonderful!*"

The only other thing it *could* have been was a boy, Merve reflected sourly. The chances were almost exactly fifty-fifty. This idiot wonderment was almost more than he could stomach, especially on top of all that he'd put up with already.

It wasn't that he disliked Miranda, or had resented her unheralded arrival, pregnant, on their doorstep. On the contrary, he quite liked the girl, and during the long hours when the two of them were alone together, with the others all out at work, they got on famously. Being left in Miranda's company was the nearest thing to being left alone that you could hope to find this side of Paradise. She didn't bother him in any way at all, neither waking him before midday, nor trying to tell him her troubles; nor even asking how the book was going. And if she ever felt bored during the long, silent afternoons of dust-laden August heat, she had the decency not to tell him so. There is nothing so disturbing to creative genius as someone else's boredom.

Yes, Miranda was O.K. Her pregnancy was O.K. too, as far as Merve was concerned; he had nothing against unmarried motherhood, or indeed any other kind. Even the baby might turn out to be O.K., for all Merve knew to the contrary.

But what was *not* O.K., and hadn't been, right from the very beginning, was the way the rest of them had chosen to act towards their new flatmate: it made him feel quite sick, though of course he'd never dare say so. It was like a mixture of worshipping the Virgin Mary and fussing over a geranium cutting, he sometimes reflected sourly, as he listened to the soft, fluting patter about the baby this and the baby that, the baby, the baby, the baby, on and on, evening after evening, while he was trying to work. And then there was Tim, with his worried, semi-professional frownings and questionings whenever he happened along —really, it was enough to get on *anyone's* nerves, even if they *weren't* trying to write a novel about life as it really is.

And now this! Naturally, Merve had accepted the fact that the whole thing was going to end, sooner or later, in a baby. That was inevitable, and in no way Miranda's fault. You couldn't blame *her* for the whole tedious business being the way it was, because that's how it had been for millions of years, in accordance with evolutionary forces which presumably knew what they were about, or if they didn't it was no use Merve complaining.

But all the same, why *now?* And why like *this?* Such a fuss, such a chattering! Such a banging of doors, such a stampeding of footsteps, such a clamouring of shrill, feminine voices, swooping, rising, falling, like gulls when the catch is in . . .

Or do *all* babies arrive like this, roughshod over everyone's convenience, in this disruptive, time-consuming and nerve-jangling manner, laying waste everyone's plans and scrunching work routines underfoot like so much spilled sugar . . . ?

Once again, Merve found himself wondering what the hell Evolution thought it was at, launching such a process on the biosphere without a word of consultation with any of the creatures involved? Again, he got no answer. Moodily, he stared some more at his blank sheet of paper, and there was no answer there, either.

Birth, copulation, and death: are not these the very stuff of all great writing? So why is it that not one of the three, when they actually occur in real life, is in the least compatible with getting anything written at all, great or otherwise?

God, what a night! Although the flat was quiet enough now, this morning, with all of them off to work at last, Merve still shuddered at the recollection of how it had been. Just after nine in the evening it had started, and at first, he'd paid no attention. He'd heard the outer door slam, and ignored it; he'd heard the uprush of chatter, like a thousand starlings; but no sooner had he succeeded in ignoring this, too, than the door of his room was flung open and they were upon him, cutting a swathe of elephants through every idea he had ever had . . .

"Swathe" of elephants, indeed! Thus had they succeeded in mucking up and making nonsense of that marvellous metaphor that had been shimmering on the edge of his consciousness just before the moment of impact. *Now* look at it . . . !

"A girl!" "A *girl,* Merve!" "Oh, Merve, *listen!*—Miranda's had a girl!" "A *girl!* Miranda's had . . . !"

Miranda, Miranda, Miranda.

A girl, a girl, a girl.

So what? So what? So what?

Gritting his teeth, and lifting his fingers from the typewriter keys, Merve tried to be nice about it.

It had gone on half the night: and then this morning, long before his usual hour, Merve had been wrenched out of deep sleep by a renewed caterwauling over some further message which some telephone-owning neighbour had brought hot-foot to their door before eight in the morning.

"*Tomorrow?* Oh, how super!" someone bellowed—voices always seem so painfully loud when you've only just woken: and then someone else (Alison, by the sound of it) shrieked something about some pink nylon net at Jones's Sale, and about doing the gathers this evening . . .

God! What was the *point* of having no telephone if this sort of thing could still happen?

The outer door slammed; and slammed again. That must be the last of them, for there were no more voices. But the air still rocked with the haste and purposefulness of them all. Further attempt to sleep was futile; there was nothing for it but to get up—actually *up*—while it was as yet barely nine in the morning.

Even now, it was only ten. Bleary-eyed, and with consciousness returning as painfully as blood into frostbitten fingers, Merve had made himself a mug of coffee, and was now sitting sluggishly in front of his manuscript, adding a comma here, scrubbing an adjective there. But it was no use. It never was at this sort of unearthly hour. His wavering genius needed time to recover from the ravages of a healthy night's sleep. It had to be humoured like a crotchety invalid, coaxed back to consciousness gently, compassionately, and by gradual stages. It needed time, it needed coffee, it needed solitude.

Sighing, Merve turned back to the bit he'd written yesterday, before all the commotion had begun. He tried to recapture the sense of excitement, the stirring of creative power, with which he had launched into the tense and dramatic scene in which Henry falls into the clutches of the predatory older woman who was to drive him, had he but known it (if he *had*, of course, many thousands of words would have been saved, but then where would have been the story line?) to the verge of suicide. Black-haired, black-eyed, blasé, and sophisticated to the *n*th degree, and with a creamy olive skin smooth as a something-or-other, not peach, too hackneyed, she'd found herself strangely fascinated by Henry's unspoiled youth and innocence . . .

"Strangely" was the word. Would *any* woman, however predatory, find herself anything other than bored through the floor by unspoiled youth and innocence on this sort of scale? Why couldn't Henry *say* something, for God's sake? Something witty and amusing, preferably, to make this creature's continued interest at least plausible?

Hell, why should he? Surely a fictional character (unlike his less fortunate counterpart in real life) should be entitled to turn to his author for a helping hand in this sort of all too familiar impasse?

"Fascinated by Henry's witty and amusing conversation," Merve wrote, "Myrtle (query Alicia?) allowed a small smile to soften the corners of her thin, harshly painted lips . . ." At which crucial moment, her creator became aware of a small sound.

Hell! Had one or other of them not gone to work after all? Just when he thought he really had got the flat to himself at last, with even Miranda out of the way? Which of them was it, and what did she think she was doing, knocking off work before eleven in the morning? What a way to run a country! Bloody bunch of skivers . . . !

Hearing his father's familiar expostulations running through his own head like this was unnerving, and only went to show what a state he was in, with all these disruptions and upheavals. Really, it was too much! He found himself literally trembling at the enormity of the decision that now confronted him. Should he go and say "hullo" straight away to whoever it was, and get it over with, or should he stay doggo in here, in the hopes of missing the salutation altogether? The trouble with this last tactic was that though it might easily work—people often popped in and out without exchanging a word if they happened to be busy—it also easily mightn't. If the intruder (for thus he viewed the fellow lodger who had invaded *his* part of the day) felt like exchanging a word with him, then exchange it she would; he was a sitting duck, in here with his typewriter, with no locks on the doors, and all this bloody togetherness thing, which worked out so well financially, but so badly on the spiritual level, or when you wanted to fry kippers in the pan they kept for bacon . . .

Waiting on tenterhooks lest someone come and say "Hullo" to you is every bit as disturbing as having them actually come and say it. Flinging caution to the winds, Merve took two strides towards the door—and then once more came to a halt. An awful thought had struck him.

Suppose it was *Miranda* out there, complete with baby! What should he *say*? What should he *do*? Merve had never spoken to a baby in his life, let alone one only a day old; and as to Miranda, he envisaged her as mysteriously and absolutely changed. A *mother*, now, just as his own mother was; a totally different category of being, and wholly outside his ken. For a full minute he stood there, in a state of pitiable and abject terror: though what, exactly, he thought Miranda might do to him, or the baby either, he could not have explained.

Gradually, though, common sense began to seep in round the edges of his panic, and a certain cautious optimism. "Forty-eight hours!" someone had shouted during this morning's bedlam, and the cry had been taken up: "Forty-eight hours . . . !" "Only forty-eight hours, isn't that super . . . ?" At the time, more than half asleep, Merve hadn't bothered to make sense of the joyous, reiterated cry: but it was clear enough now. Miranda and the baby were to stay in hospital for forty-eight hours, of which—yippee!—not much more than twelve had as yet elapsed! It *couldn't* be Miranda.

Emboldened by this thought, but still wary, Merve put his head round the door and listened. From the kitchen, he could hear the faint but unmistakable clink of crockery. The dresser drawer was opened, and then closed. The delicious aroma of fresh coffee, made from freshly ground beans, began to fill the air.

It was Iris. This much he might have guessed, actually, she being the only one who ever took the trouble to make coffee in the proper way. Wearing a sleeveless dress of brown and white striped cotton, very crisp and trim, she was sitting at the kitchen table sipping black coffee from one of the Wedgwood mugs, and studying with quiet intensity the newspaper outspread in front of her.

She looked up as Merve came in.

"Hullo: coffee?" she offered pleasantly, gesturing towards the percolator still bubbling softly: and then, as he clattered around finding himself mug, spoon, sugar, evaporated milk, she continued smoothly: "I suppose you've heard that the proud Mum will be back in residence tomorrow? Complete with offspring?"

Merve nodded dumbly. How could he not have heard? And heard, too, until his ears rattled with it, how the child had blue eyes, fair hair, and weighed nine and a half pounds—an exceptional weight, apparently, judging by the chirrups of awe and admiration that had accompanied the statistic, though in fact it wasn't much heavier than an average sort of cat.

Was Iris really planning to tell him all this *again* . . . ! Oh, God . . . !

But Iris, when she spoke, seemed to be talking more to herself than to him.

"The silly girl! There was no need for it to have weighed *that* much!" she remarked softly, with a sort of dry amusement; and Merve, momentarily startled out of his boredom, very nearly asked her what on earth she meant.

But he stopped himself just in time. She would only have answered, and then there he'd have been, with a *conversation* on his hands, the very thing he'd been trying so earnestly to avoid. Conversation was endemic in this place and, if you let it, would gobble up every moment of your free time, every ounce of your emotional energy. It would somehow lap up and trivialise the best and brightest of your creative ideas, nourishing itself on them like some gigantic spiritual tapeworm.

So Merve said nothing; just got himself out of the kitchen as rapidly as possible, slopping coffee over the edge of the mug as he went. And Iris, after giving him a swift, pitying glance, said nothing either.

For she, too, was preoccupied this morning. Carefully, she selected from the morning's newspapers such pages as she was going to need, and tucked them into the back of the dresser drawer. She was neat and precise in all her movements, for she was an orderly person by nature—as indeed she needed to be, for these chaotic, free-and-easy households can only survive if somewhere in the background there is a clear and disciplined intelligence in charge. Without this, they will disintegrate within a week.

But Iris had not taken the whole day off from her fairly demanding job just to read the papers. There was a lot that she had to get through yet, one of the items involving a journey of a good many miles, right across London, and she was particularly anxious to be back in plenty of time to listen to the News.

And in plenty of time she was: though, as it turned out, there were no fresh revelations so far about the stolen baby. At the end of the News, a psychiatrist was brought on to pontificate (Iris's word, when she was discussing the programme afterwards with Tim) about these "Crimes of Love" as he dubbed them, giving it as his professional (and not very startling) opinion that girls who steal babies are themselves the victims of a desperate need for love. They see the baby, with its unquestioning, passionate dependence on whoever cares for it, as a love object par excellence with which to fill the aching void, and they deserve pity rather than blame, support and sympathy rather than punishment. Very often (he pointed out) they have suffered some recent trauma of loss or desertion, and have received neither sympathy nor understanding from their families, from whom indeed they may be quite alienated. Compassion, not severity, must be the keynote in dealing with such a victim of her own desperate compulsions, and he appealed to Miss X, whoever she might be, to come forward and give herself up. If she brought the baby back safe and sound, he assured her, she would have nothing to fear; sympathy, understanding, and practical help with her problems would be forthcoming in full measure. And he finished by declaring that it was Society that was to blame, not the unhappy baby-snatcher herself. We are all guilty, because if someone needs love *that* desperately, then clearly it is someone's duty to love them . . .

Iris's lip curled, and she reached towards the knob. Love as a matter of duty was something that she'd seen in action, and she was all too familiar with the place to which it led.

CHAPTER 15

Miss X was listening to the talk, too, her radio turned down very low. Unlike Iris, she found nothing to mock at in the psychiatrist's benign if slightly platitudinous utterances. Almost every word of it struck home to her with poignant accuracy: the desperate hunger for love—the alienation from an uncomprehending family—the recent shattering trauma—why, the man was describing *her*, and so exactly that for a few mad seconds she imagined that he must somehow have tracked her down, and at any moment was going to reveal her identity to all the world.

But he didn't; and hearing herself described, instead, as "Miss X," she felt a rush of absurd relief—even, indeed, a mischievous little flutter of excitement!

"Miss X!"—What fun! What a wonderful anonymous feeling it gave her! Irresponsible, too! She felt her past self slipping away, and this Miss X emerging like a snake from its skin into a new and shining world.

"How wonderful it is to be
Just Miss X instead of me!"

she crooned softly to the little creature in her arms, sleeping so peacefully, so trustfully, and with no notion of not belonging there. She looked down at the small, unconscious face, and felt herself drowning in protective love. What should she teach the child to call her, as the months rolled forward bringing it to the verge of speech, to the brink of understanding?

Not "Mummy," that was for sure. The associations were far too painful.

The baby stirred in her arms, screwing up its face into a thousand wrinkles, and Miss X looked around for somewhere to lay it down while she prepared the bottle. She should have improvised a crib of some kind, not to mention a proper stock of essentials, such as disposable nappies and tins of Cow and Gate, before ever embarking on this wild venture—but then, how could she have known?

It had all happened so suddenly: or so it had seemed at the time. It was only now, twenty-four hours later, that she realised that it hadn't actually been sudden at all, but had been growing, invisibly and imperceptibly, in her empty, broken heart, ever since the blow had first fallen.

The pram had been parked so carelessly, so hurriedly on the hot pavement outside the supermarket, without even the brakes on properly, and in the full glare of the August sun. Miss X had watched the mother, a blowsy, angry-looking woman of forty or more, yanking her grizzling three-year-old away from the pram, and dragging him, whiny and miserable, into the crowded store. She did not give so much as a backward glance at the pram, though by now its occupant, roused by the sudden cessation of movement, had begun to whimper.

Miss X waited while the whimpering sharpened, gathered power, and finally escalated to full-blown yelling. Then, after a quick, nervous glance at the store's entrance to see if the mother was returning, she stepped nearer: one more cautious glance around, and she was leaning down over the pram and peering in under the hood.

A very young baby, still pink with newness, like an opening rose, flailed its tiny arms into the vastness of the universe, and howled its needs into the unknown.

Miss X straightened up and stepped backwards with guilty haste, though as yet her intention was barely lapping the fringes of her conscious mind. She stood, uneasily, a yard or so away, quite expecting the mother to return at any moment. Surely these passionate yells of rage and despair would have reached *any* mother's ears, no matter how great the press of crowds and noise in there?

A minute passed . . . and another. It was all nonsense what that mother had said, later, to the police, about having left the baby for only a couple of minutes. It was five at least, if not more; she'd almost screamed this fact right into the television screen when she heard the woman lying like that, but had stopped herself just in time.

It was impossible just to stand by, listening to those screams, and doing absolutely nothing. Miss X could hold back no longer. With a sense of coming home at last, she leaned down, down, into the warm recesses under the hood, and gathered into her arms the quivering, furious little creature.

Instantly, as if she had turned some magic switch, the cries ceased, and were replaced by contented little sucking sounds. The warm, lovely little weight slumped in utter trust against her unfamiliar shoulder as if that was where it had always belonged, and she felt herself drowning in total, unquestioning love, though whether it was hers or the baby's she could not possibly have told. She was filled, overwhelmed, by a sense of the golden, absolute rightness of what she was doing, and clutching the child close against her chilled, awakening bosom, she whipped round the corner and away.

She could not believe it, at first, that no one was running after her; that no angry shouts, no startled eyes, bulging with accusation, were following her: *You're* not a real mother, *you're* just a thief and an imposter, a withered branch, a dried-up water-hole! *That's* not your baby, anyone can see it isn't! That's a *real* baby, and you are but barren stock . . .

But no goggling eyes, no cries of outrage were pursuing her. No one seemed to remark her at all as she walked fast, but not too fast, down the almost empty side-street

. . . round the corner at the bottom . . . and into an even emptier one, drowsy with the long afternoon's heat. No heads leaned out of windows as she passed, no faces peered round the lace curtains. A cat licked itself on a dusty, baking doorstep; and old woman watered her geraniums; a young coloured boy, carrying a ladder, passed, whistling, on the other side of the road.

"Nah, leave it, man, leave it!" someone admonished wearily from inside one of the upstairs rooms; and gradually, bit by bit, it was borne in upon Miss X that no one was taking any notice of her at all: that the world was still simply going about its business, just as if nothing had happened.

By the time she reached the park she was really tired, glad to sit down in the coolness under one of the great trees. Still no one was staring at her, and if they glanced in her direction at all, it was only with that mild, benevolent interest that the sight of a baby in arms sometimes arouses in women who have had children of their own, especially those who are now past having any more.

"How old is the little dear?" asked the comfortable, bespectacled Gran who was sitting on the bench next her; and for a moment, Miss X felt a horrid little twinge of alarm. How old *was* the baby? Very young, almost newborn, she'd guessed; but suppose she'd guessed wrong? Suppose her companion, suddenly and terrifyingly knowledgeable (on the basis, perhaps, of thirteen children of her own and countless nephews, nieces, grandchildren)—suppose she were to peer closer into the baby's face, and then, puzzled and suspicious, turn upon Miss X and say . . .

But she didn't. On the contrary, she didn't even seem to notice that her question hadn't been answered.

"Aah!" she said, laying down her knitting to smile and cluck her tongue at the sleeping infant. "Aah, they're lovely at this age, aren't they, dear? Pity they have to grow up!"—and then, clucking some more and beaming even closer into the baby's face, she continued, innocently as ever:

"Lovely, isn't he?—Or is it a little girl?"

And it was only now, for the very first time, that it dawned on Miss X that she hadn't the faintest idea. Somehow it hadn't occurred to her that her prize could be other than female, simply because this was what she so passionately wanted it to be. But of course you couldn't really tell just by their faces, not at this age.

Just wait a moment, and I'll have a look—Miss X had to suppress a hysterical giggle as the only straightforward and honest answer flashed through her mind. Then, pulling herself together, she took the plunge.

"A little girl," she said boldly, and felt a surge of fear at thus tempting Providence; and then a surge of wild longing to go home straight away, undress the child, and find out for sure . . .

Home? She must be out of her mind! Bidding the old lady a hasty good-bye, she heaved herself to her feet, and clutching the unprotesting little bundle close to her, she hurried across the grass until she reached the shelter of a little clump of bushes alongside the Ladies. There, half-hidden in the long grass, she sat down with the baby in her lap and began, with trembling fingers, to pick her way through the plethora of lower garments—poor little thing, far too many layers of wool and nylon for a day like this!—until she reached at last the soaked, steaming nappy—an old-fashioned towelling one, fastened with two large safety pins, savage and gigantic alongside the tiny thighs.

One pin . . . Two pins . . .

A *girl!* So she *had* been right! Although the chances of being right had been every bit as good as the chances of being wrong, it seemed to Miss X like a sign from Heaven, a direct message from God himself that this truly *was* her baby. By guessing right, she had actually made it her own! Male and female created he them, but she,

Miss X, had managed at will to create female only, simply by saying so! "A little girl," she had told the old woman, boldly and uncompromisingly, thus bringing into being this tiny, pink female crease between the tirelessly pedalling thighs.

"Let it be a girl!" she had commanded; and it *was* a girl!

Strange that she, who hadn't thought about religion in years, and had certainly never believed in miracles, should suddenly find herself in possession of such powers!

CHAPTER 16

The forty-eight hours were over, and Miranda was due back at the Squat that very evening.

Everything was ready. The pink nylon net had been bought, and gathered into a pretty frill round the borrowed crib with its second-hand sheets and blankets, lovingly washed and ironed. A patchwork quilt, all pinks and mauves and tiny white flowers, had been donated by the sister-in-law of one of the girls in Alison's office, and was now draped in readiness over the end of the crib, the washed-out colours and slightly frayed seams blurred into an all-over radiance by the evening sun. All the members of the Squat—even Merve—were gathered round, as if at some shrine, awed and expectant, while out in the kitchen the celebration dinner—one of Iris's special goulashes, with garlic and red peppers—was gently simmering.

"Just imagine—Baby Caroline will be actually *here*—actually *this evening!*" murmured Alison, gazing wonderingly into the waiting crib. "Fancy—her little golden head against the white—"

"It won't be golden," Iris was beginning, "new-born babies are always . . ." but Alison seemed not to have heard. ". . . against the white pillowcase," she continued, as if there had been no interruption. "I'm glad it was the white ones your cousin sent us in the end, Belinda, and not the yellow. For a very fair baby, yellow would be awful . . ."

"And unlucky, too," put in Belinda. "Yellow's one of the unlucky colours. Not as bad as green, of course, but not too good . . . I warned her at the time—my cousin—not to buy them, but she wouldn't listen, and sure enough Jonathan got this awful rash when he was only five weeks old . . . all over his tummy and bottom, and it must have been horribly itchy, because he cried and cried, they got no sleep for the best part of a week. She couldn't say I hadn't warned her. It's the middle band of the spectrum, you see: the red end's all right, and the blue end's all right, but in the middle—*No,* Tim, it's *not* nonsense! Even the scientists are beginning to accept the idea that colours can affect things. They did this experiment with school classrooms—I was reading about it only recently—with some of the classrooms painted blue—I think it was—and the others orange: and they found that the children in the orange classrooms . . ."

"Shush!" Alison's voice was shrill and urgent—"Listen—isn't that a taxi drawing up outside?"—and they all rushed to the window.

But it wasn't. They drew back their craning necks and returned to waiting stations. A little querulous now, from the mounting tension, they resumed the conversation from where it broke off. Somebody pointed out that if there were indeed some parts of the spectrum that were unluckier than others, then white must be the unluckiest of all, since in it were contained *all* the colours.

Naturally, Belinda wasn't going to give in that easily. After barely a moment's hesitation, she managed to recall yet another article she'd read, in the *Scientific American*, or *Amazing Predictions*, or somewhere, to the effect that . . .

Alison, almost in tears, struggled to shut them all up and restore the mood of almost religious ecstasy with which the vigil had begun.

"Oh, *please* don't let's be having a stupid fight about nothing just when Miranda's coming home!" she wailed. "Just imagine—for Baby Caroline—if the first human words she hears are a silly argument about spectrums—Oh, *all right*, 'spectra' if you like!—That's just exactly the sort of thing I mean! Look, let's drop all this, and talk about the baby, shall we?"—here she glared ferociously round the little circle, daring any of them to challenge this switch to holier ground—"Oh, I do so wonder what she'll be *like*, don't you. Of course, we know she's fair, and her blue eyes and everything: but I mean what she's actually *like*? . . . You know . . . ?"

Iris listened to the idle, baseless speculations that were being tossed to and fro; and now and then allowed a tiny pitying smile to curl her lips, when none of them were looking.

For she, and she alone, actually *knew* what the small face would be like which was so soon to nestle on that pillow: for had she not seen photographs of it, by the dozen, in every single newspaper, ever since yesterday morning?

And she alone, likewise, knew what was going to be wrong with the child.

Because, of course, the baby which Miranda, all starry-eyed and maternal, was going to lay reverently in that crib, was not going to be a new-born baby at all, but one turned three weeks old.

With secret, growing impatience, which was like a sort of greed, Iris savoured the coming scenario.

Alison, Belinda, and Merve would, of course, be taken in completely. "Gosh, isn't she *big!*" one of them might exclaim admiringly: but that sly little cow had already forestalled that line of thinking by announcing that the baby had weighed nine and a half pounds at birth—quite unnecessary, actually, since a new baby actually *loses* weight for its first few days, and by three weeks may have done little more than catch up to its original weight. But Miranda wouldn't know this.

Tim would, though. After all those years of medical

training, let alone having just recently got through his midwifery course with flying colours, he could hardly fail to be familiar with so basic a fact. He would be familiar, too, with the differences that *do* exist between a newborn baby and one that is three weeks old. If not at first glance, then certainly the moment he picked it up, he would know. He would recognise at once that indefinable firmness of texture, that solidity of contour, which three weeks' exposure to the great outside world gives to the limp, tacky body of the newborn. He would feel the already purposeful thrust of the maturing muscles in the tiny, and yet no longer stick-like, limbs; he would see the eyes, wide open, and already trying to focus; and he would *know*. He could not help knowing.

And if, somehow, he *did* fail to recognise these signs, then Iris would lose no time in enlightening him. And this alternative scenario, as it took shape in her mind, was in some ways even more delicious than the first.

"Goodness, fancy her eyes being so wide open, as if she was really *looking* at you!" Iris envisaged herself saying innocently: and, "Good heavens, how *strong* she is! Just feel, Tim!—did you ever feel muscles like that on a newborn baby? . . ." "And her skin so rosy and firm . . . no redness . . . no wrinkles . . ." On and on she would pile the apparently innocent compliments, from the shape of the child's head—"Fancy, no moulding!"—to the strength of its cry, and the confident vigour of its search for breast or bottle, its general air, in short, of having already learned the tricks of its trade. She pictured the bewilderment on Tim's face . . . the slow dawning of suspicion . . . and then, finally, the utter shock as the truth hit him: the horror, dismay, and revulsion . . .

Iris felt the black jealousy of the last few weeks subsiding. The celebration bottle of wine Tim had brought in winked in the sunset light; and Iris almost winked back.

She could hardly wait for it all to begin.

Trying to get the baby dressed that afternoon, Miss X had found herself a bag of nerves, terrified of every creaking board, even of every passing footstep in the street.

Until now, she had been sustained by a sort of euphoria, compounded of delight in her new little companion, and triumph at having got away with it: of having outwitted the lot of them! A dozen times a day, turned down as low as a whisper, she would listen to the news of her crime, gloating over every false trail, every misleading clue that the police were so painstakingly investigating.

Sometimes, seething with secret mischief, she felt an almost uncontrollable impulse to tease them a little; to play Hunt the Thimble with them, as at children's parties long ago: "Colder . . . colder . . . bit warmer now . . . Ah, colder again! . . . *ice*-cold . . . *free-eezing!*"—laughing behind her hand as they stumbled this way and that in accordance with her directions, sometimes veering in the right direction, more often in the wrong . . . Wrong . . . wrong . . . wronger . . . !

It was an impulse that must be resisted, of course. Probably most successful criminals are assailed by it at times—"Ha-ha! Sold again! *This* is how I did it, you silly goons . . . !"—but this way disaster lies. Miss X, like so many another malefactor, must keep her cleverness to herself.

And she *had* been clever; there could be no doubt about that. To have thought of this hiding place, so obvious, and yet so cunningly camouflaged as to put absolutely *everyone* off the scent—this had been a stroke of genius. In contemplating her own ingenuity, and silently congratulating herself upon it, Miss X felt her panic subsiding, and she applied herself once more to getting the baby into its clean clothes. She yearned to have something prettier than these old things to dress the little girl in, but of course it was impossible. It would be madness to be caught shopping for baby clothes at just this juncture; probably every mother-and-baby outfitters in London had been alerted by now, and would be keeping an eye open for new and suspicious customers.

Never mind. It wasn't going to be for long, and meanwhile these second-hand oddments were better than nothing: better, certainly, than the thick, wintry woollies that the child's former mother had put on her. Miss X had lost no time in getting rid of *those*, and not only because they could prove incriminating. She wanted also to get rid of every trace of the child's former life and thus make it totally hers. Above all, she intended to get rid of the ridiculous Christian name it had been burdened with—"Dawn," of all things—did you ever hear of anything so affected and soppy? And even worse, "My Dawnie," as the woman was wont to say when interviewed by the Press.

Leaning close, Miss X tried to whisper to the baby its new name, the lovely old family name she'd had in mind from the very beginning, or even before: but, as always when she came to pronounce the syllables, memory surged back, and she found herself choked with tears.

But this was no time for sentiment: there was a lot still to be done. When the last of the waving little pink limbs had been inserted into the faded cotton romper suit several sizes too large, Miss X laid the child in the crib she had by now improvised out of a cardboard box, and hurried to prepare a bottle—by no means an easy task in this neglected and somewhat unhygienic place, where nothing seemed to work, and water ran brown from the taps. Even getting the milk to the right temperature was quite a problem, let alone sterilizing bottle and teat; and all the time there was the fear that the baby might start crying before she was ready. This had been the biggest hazard all along, and though Miss X had worked out an ingenious way of tackling it, it wasn't really a satisfactory way, nor particularly pleasant for the baby. Each time,

Miss X hated doing it, and could only hope that the procedure wouldn't end up giving the child a complex, or something.

Still, it wasn't going to be for long. Soon, all these precautions would be a thing of the past.

Seven o'clock . . . eight o'clock . . . and still Miranda hadn't returned to the Squat. The sun had long gone off the pink-frilled crib, leaving it pallid and tatty-looking. The goulash was slowly spoiling in the oven, and the reception committee was growing anxious and restive.

"I *told* you one of us should have gone and fetched her," Tim grumbled; and Iris reminded him, rather sharply, that Miranda had particularly requested that this should not be done, ringing up the next-door people specially with a message to this effect.

"Don't you remember, I told you, she said she'd been moved to an annexe, or something, she wasn't sure exactly where . . . ?"

"You could have found out," Tim retorted. "It's not all that difficult to . . ." But before Iris had time to retaliate, a little squeal from Alison brought them all to their feet.

"A car . . . ! I can hear it slowing down!" she shrieked; and once again there was a stampede to the window—only to find that the car was indeed slowing down, but only preparatory to turning the corner at the end of the road.

"Let's eat," proposed Merve, sniffing hungrily at the aroma of soon-to-be-ruined goulash; and while the party were still debating this heartless suggestion—more and more favourably as the minutes passed—a slight noise from outside brought the chatter to an abrupt halt.

There in the doorway stood Miranda, slim, white-faced, and quite alone.

"She's dead. Baby Caroline is dead," she announced, calmly and firmly; then flung herself onto the sofa, sobbing as if her grief would never end.

CHAPTER 17

They were all absolutely stunned, and for several seconds no one spoke at all. Then, in two strides, Tim was across the room and kneeling by the stricken girl. Iris had to stand by and watch his arms going round the barefaced little fraud, listen to his voice murmuring condolences for the phoney bereavement into her damp, wild hair.

"Oh, my dear . . . ! Oh, Miranda, love, how absolutely *awful* for you! But remember, you've still got *us* . . . We're all here . . . we're all going to help you . . ."—and then, a little later—"you wouldn't like, would you, love, to tell us how it happened . . . ? Talk about it . . ."

No, she wouldn't. By hunched shoulders, and a small shake of her head half-buried in cushions, Miranda indicated as much, and Tim did not press her, nor allow any of the others to do so. Later, when Miranda was at last in bed and asleep, drugged into unconsciousness by a heavy dose of sleeping pills, he harangued the others almost as if it was all their fault.

"On *no* account is anyone to question her, or worry her in any way," he ordered, his voice taut and peremptory with concern, "especially you girls—I know what you are, I know you're all wild with curiosity—and come to that, so am I. I'm not going to rest, I assure you, until I've found out exactly what did happen, and who's responsible—but not by asking the poor kid herself! She's in a state of shock. Do you understand—*no one* is to ask her anything at all, or bother her in any way whatsoever. Is that clear . . . ?"

Iris's face was like stone. The sharp, almost accusatory words seemed as if they were addressed specifically to her—and indeed, this was in a sense the case. The three younger ones were all of them too limp, in their various ways, to serve as targets for his anger and bewilderment. Belinda and Alison, weeping softly, were way out of reach in a sad little world of wasted pink frills and unfulfilled knitting. Silently, tearfully, they had dismantled the pretty little crib, pushed out of sight the toys and the lovingly assembled small garments, and now there was nothing left to do but cry, quietly and uselessly, until they were tired enough to sleep. And as to Merve, embarrassed and guiltily conscious of mourning the goulash far more sincerely than he at all knew how to mourn a baby—he, too, was a non-starter as either scapegoat or confidante. In his decorously downcast eyes, you could already see the stirrings of calculation: how soon, after a tragedy like this, could you decently start typing? There were no precedents to go by, for in the course of his short and boring life no one had ever died, nothing tragic had ever happened, and so he longed above all things to know how *long*, for God's sake, it all had to *last?* It wasn't even as if any of the unfortunate episode could be salvaged and recycled for Henry's benefit, or for Myrtle (query Alicia). It just simply wasn't Henry's scene, or Myrtle-Alicia's either. Even if she *did* have a baby (which would have been terribly out of character as well as biologically improbable at her age, and would have mucked up the plot beyond redemption) and even if she thereafter lost it (a worse departure still from the projected script, and even less Alicia's thing than having one) he simply could see no way of handling all this crying over pink knitting wool and stuff. Alicia just wouldn't: she'd be every bit as relieved as her harassed author to be rid of the superfluous little creature on the earliest page possible.

The whole evening, clearly, was going to be a dead

loss: six hours down the drain. And to what purpose? It was rotten luck on Miranda, of course it was, and if Merve's not doing any typing would have brought the baby back to life, then he wouldn't have grudged it for one moment, he wasn't *that* heartless.

How heartless, actually, *was* he, then? Searching this heart of his for clues, it began to appear that he hadn't got one, or anyway he couldn't find it. From ribs to belly to backbone, there seemed to be nothing but a vast, gaping void.

Unnoticed, and certainly un-missed, Merve crept softly from the room. Tiptoeing into the kitchen, he extracted from the oven the blackened goulash and hurried it furtively into his room, closing the door softly but decisively behind him.

There were quite a few good bits left, if you poked around. Employing in turn knife, spoon, razor blade, nail file, and scissors, Merve scooped and scraped with mounting success and gusto, but silently, and with a sort of respectful intensity, as befitted a house of mourning . . .

It was past midnight, and Iris had been alone for over an hour. The other girls had gone to bed, or she supposed they had; they'd drifted out of the room, anyway, and she'd heard nothing from them since. Merve, too, must be asleep, or having Writers' Block, or something, for there was no sound from his room, either.

It was Tim she was waiting up for: Tim, who, having brusquely demanded of her all the 2p coins she'd got, had rushed out into the night to telephone non-existent hospitals and imaginary obstetricians.

He couldn't say she hadn't tried to warn him. "Wait, Tim, there's something I want to tell you . . ." she'd cautiously begun; but, "For God's sake—!" he'd interrupted impatiently, and then, "Is this *all*?—" glaring accusingly at the scant collection of 2p pieces she'd managed to unearth from her handbag.

So, O.K., *be* like that, she'd responded, but not aloud. If he *wanted* to waste his time and make a fool of himself on hospital switchboards the length and breadth of London . . .

She hadn't bothered to draw the curtains, and now the big naked windows loomed black and vast. The shadowy room, lit by a single unshaded bulb, looked shabby and desolate; the old floorboards and the neglected woodwork creaked and sighed as they shrank and settled after the heat of the day.

Iris stirred in the big chair, and glanced at her watch. The wild goose chase seemed to be taking him longer than she'd supposed. But never mind. There wasn't any hurry. There was no way, now, that she wasn't going to win.

Of course, it couldn't now be quite the same scene as she'd planned. This had been fouled-up completely and forever by the extraordinary turn events had taken—Iris was still trying to work out the implications of it all.

In one sense, it hadn't been extraordinary at all: indeed, up till a couple of days ago, she had taken for granted that Miranda would do just exactly what she had today done: that is, turn up as if butter wouldn't melt in her mouth, and announce that the baby was dead. It was difficult to see what else the girl *could* do, and Iris's only doubt had been whether to reveal to Tim his protégé's monstrous perfidy before or after this dénouement.

But that was before the news of the stolen baby had hit the headlines. From then on, the prospect was absolutely changed—on the face of it, for the better: because now there was a dreadful crime to lay at Miranda's door, on top of the lying and the treachery.

Iris's glee had been unbounded. Her big scene was going to be even bigger than she'd anticipated. Miranda would go to prison, or Borstal, or a mental home, or somewhere, and Tim, in his shock and disillusionment, would turn for comfort to his old love . . .

What the *hell* was taking him so long? Surely it didn't take half the night to ascertain that there was no such hospital as St. Benedict's? Or, if by chance there was, that it had never had on its maternity list any such patient as Miranda Field . . . ?

Ah, but here perhaps was a clue. Iris had almost forgotten that it was she, and she alone, who knew the secret of Miranda's surname. Well, not "secret," exactly; it was just that among the unspoken house rules of the Squat was one that ordained that no one should ever be pressed for his or her true identity if they showed the slightest reluctance to reveal it. This kind of carefully nurtured ignorance not only made for mutual trust and goodwill, but served as a useful first line of defence against the Squat's natural enemies—parents and such. There is nothing so convincing as the truth, and "I'm sorry, we don't know anyone of that name" *was* the truth so long as everyone kept to these unwritten rules.

Iris herself had come across Miranda's surname by the merest chance. She hadn't been looking for it. What had motivated her quick, furtive prowl round the girl's bedroom, while its owner was having a bath, had been sheer curiosity as to what was being used as padding under that maternity smock. It was in the course of this hasty investigation that she'd come across the school sandals, and had happened to notice the smudged, inked-in letters along the underside of the strap: "M. FIELD, FORM IVA," and had filed away the information in her mind for future reference. When the crunch came, as sooner or later it must, this was a bit of data that was going to come in useful—and, by God, it had! It had taken Iris almost one whole morning to work through one and a half columns of Fields in the telephone directory, but it had been a morning well spent. The wary male voice which had finally admitted to owning a daugher named Miranda had sounded absolutely terrified.

The cards, then, were all in Iris's hands by now, to play exactly as she chose. Victory was certain. Only the timing was still in doubt, and how best to deploy the carefully assembled evidence so as to maximise her rival's humiliation.

Her rival. Iris hated to accord Miranda such status, even in the secret places of her own brain; but no other word sprang to mind. It was only now, with her own total triumph clearly in sight, that Iris could allow herself to be fully aware of the black, savage jealousy that had been consuming her ever since that first moment when Tim, bubbling over with asinine awe and admiration, had introduced this fraudulent little cow into their midst. And he a nearly qualified doctor, too! How blind can you get?

Well, love is blind, or so they say; though Iris herself had never found this to be so. On the contrary, it was just when she loved most deeply that she'd always found herself most agonisingly aware of the flaws and weaknesses in the beloved.

Still, this might not be everyone's experience; and anyway, Tim didn't actually love Miranda—or if he did, he hadn't allowed himself to be aware of it. But all the same, his enormous and misplaced concern for the wretched girl, his ridiculous admiration of her "courage," had been enough, and more than enough, to awaken the black memories: the bitter, unappeased resentment. Watching him, over these past days, lavishing upon this sly newcomer all the solicitude, all the tenderness, the concern, the admiration that should have—that *would* have—belonged to Iris, watching all this, Iris had felt the jealousy growing in her like a disease, monstrous, out of control, poisoning the very roots of her being.

It had been weeks since Tim had slept with her; the rot had set in long before Miranda's appearance on the scene.

Exams, he'd said; nights on duty, he'd said; feelings of being pressured, he'd said. And so, to make him feel less pressured, to enable him to concentrate on his exams, Iris had had her abortion.

He hadn't pushed her into it, she must give him that; but no one could mistake the look of relief on his face when she told him of her decision. And he'd gone on, in his relief, to do all the right things. He'd gone with her to the hospital, had visited with sympathy and flowers, had escorted her home again when it was over. He'd been unfailingly kind and attentive throughout, you couldn't fault his behaviour anywhere.

And all the time, while he'd been behaving so well, while he'd been doing all these right things, his real feelings, deep in his heart, had been feelings of contempt and disillusion: had he not declared as much, out loud, in front of everyone, on the evening of Miranda's arrival?

"Most girls would have chickened-out right from the start!"—these had been his very words, in tones of wonder and admiration: and it had seemed to Iris, listening quietly in the background, that there could be little doubt of the name for which "most girls" was an all too transparent euphemism.

So she, Iris, had merely "chickened-out," had she? She who had done this thing for *his* sake, to give him back his freedom, his peace of mind, his final Medical Board exam?

And, of course, to make him love her again.

"I'll give him 'chickening-out'!" she reflected grimly; and in that moment heard the outer door slam.

Slamming doors at one in the morning. They'd have the neighbours on at them again, and perhaps another complaint to the Housing Department. And now, looking ten years older, here he was. Not a word of greeting. Not a hint of apology for having been gone so long. Just Miranda, Miranda, Miranda . . .

"Not a word of sense out of any of them!" he blustered,

distraught and frightened. "No one's heard of St. Benedict's . . . I've been phoning practically every maternity outfit in London, I've been going nearly frantic, and the only bloody thing I can get out of any of them is, 'I'm sorry, but what is the patient's *surname?*' Bloody fools! You would think, wouldn't you, that a young kid like that . . . having a baby all by herself, with no husband, no relatives . . . and then losing it within forty-eight hours . . . you'd hardly need to look it up on a bloody list!"

Iris sat very still, savouring the moment. *Her* moment. It had come. Then:

"Be fair to them, Tim. She didn't lose a baby. She never had a baby. She wasn't pregnant at all, didn't you realise that? She was pretending."

She paused, waiting for a reaction. When none came, she continued; rubbing it well in:

"*I* spotted it within twenty-four hours, and I'm amazed that you didn't—you with your Honourable Mention in Midwifery, and all! Didn't it strike you as odd, the way she never seemed to . . . ? And the way she always . . . ?"

And so and so on: while Tim stood white-faced, speechless and staring.

CHAPTER 18

"You're crazy!" Tim said at last; but already he knew that she wasn't. You could see it in his slack jaw, his blank, shocked eyes.

"You're crazy!" he repeated, as if still hoping, somehow, to convince himself that it was so. But of course this couldn't happen, not with his degree of medical knowledge, and Iris's rapier skill in directing his attention to the signs and symptoms that should have alerted him. The quick, agile way Miranda moved about the place, getting up from her chair and sitting down again quite effortlessly, with no careful lowering of the big, ungainly body; no heaving of it up again with the help of both hands, leaning forwards for greater thrust. Then there was her straight back, her easy, upright posture; the spring in her step as she moved and turned. And in addition to all this, there was the exaggerated, improbable size of her abdomen—not to mention the occasional slip-up in the shape of it, especially towards evening, when she had grown careless, and tended not to notice that her day-long padding had worked round to the left a little, or to the right, as the case might be.

And as if this wasn't enough, what about all that mystery and evasiveness surrounding the hospital visits and the check-ups? The coincidence that they should happen on just the one afternoon in the week when Tim couldn't take her there? Her vagueness about what the doctor had said; her bland acceptance of his culpable inaction as the baby went more and more dangerously overdue?

Tim listened. The circumstantial evidence, assembled with such painstaking venom over so many days, added up to a case so watertight as to preclude argument; and Tim knew it. White, appalled, absolutely thrown, he stared at Iris with just that look of dawning horror, of growing revulsion and disgust, that she'd been dreaming of, day and night throughout all this long ordeal; and now, at last, it was here.

"You mean," he said at last, incredulously, "you meant that, knowing all this, you just stood by and let the poor kid sweat it out? That you did *nothing* to help or comfort her? Didn't you ever for one moment wonder what sort of hell she must be going through to resort to so desperate a deception? You never wondered *at all?* Never asked her?—never sought her confidence—never offered help, or guidance, or a shoulder to weep on? You did *nothing?* Knowing what you did, you stirred not a finger to help, but just sat there watching, like a cat watching a mouse, waiting for her to crack? What sort of a woman *are* you?"

A good question. But Iris was not the person qualified to answer it, least of all at this moment of total disorientation. Nothing in any of those delectable scenarios she'd been so gleefully conjuring up of late had prepared her for anything remotely like this, and she couldn't, at first, take it in. That the long-anticipated revulsion and horror should indeed be spreading across Tim's features exactly on schedule—but that they should be inspired not by Miranda, but by *her*, Iris . . . ! Her head swam. She could only stare dumbly at him, simply unable to piece together what she had heard.

Pride came to her aid at last. Pride, and that final trump card which she still had up her sleeve, and had been saving for the climax.

"'*Comfort* her!' Oh, I like that! Did I ever wonder what sort of a hell she was going through? you ask me: well, now I'm going to ask *you* something! Did *she* ever wonder what sort of a hell that poor mother would be going through when she found her baby missing?—Is still going through . . ."

Tim's look of blank and genuine incomprehension robbed her of the last shreds of self control. She did not wait for him to say "What mother?" but leapt to her feet, and her voice rose to a scream:

"The mother whose baby Miranda's stolen, you bloody half-baked fool!" she yelled. "Stolen, stolen, stolen! Your precious Miranda's stolen a baby! It's been in all the papers for days! Don't you ever read anything? Or watch television? Or talk to anybody? Have you gone deaf and blind and barmy rootling after those bloody exams like a pig among garbage?—a bloody chauvinist loony bloody pig . . . !"

"You're crazy!" This time, he meant it. "How could the poor kid have stolen a baby?—Hell, I mean, it doesn't make *sense!*" Confronted with the blatant non sequitur of Iris's wild accusations, his scientific training began to take precedence over his sense of outrage, and he found himself reasoning with her in an almost normal tone of voice, analysing the situation logically into its mutually contradictory parts.

"All right, so stealing someone else's baby could have looked like one of the options for a girl in her predicament. The other, and far simpler, option was to come back and say that the baby had died; and it so happens that this was the option she chose. We all know she did. We were all there; we all heard her say it, with our own ears—"

Here Iris made as if to interrupt; but he silenced her.

"O.K., so she settled for the simpler of the two options; maybe she didn't even think of the second one, but even if she did—well, for God's sake, why would she want to do *both?* If she'd stolen a baby, which is what you seem to be saying, then why in the world would she come back here saying that it's dead . . . ?"

Iris gave him a long, steady look, holding his gaze until at last his impeccable logic faltered into silence.

"Perhaps it is," she said.

CHAPTER 19

Janine was gnawing restlessly at her long, beautifully lacquered finger nails—a thing she hadn't done in years—and debating with herself, over and over, whether she dared pop in next door, here and now, before anyone else beat her to it, and reveal to poor Norah this fresh, shocking bit of news. The temptation was almost irresistible, for hadn't Janine said all along that she felt sure Miranda Field must have had something to do with this baby-snatching business? Well, no—and this was just what was so maddening about the whole thing—she *hadn't* said so, not at the time, and not in so many words; though by now she'd just about convinced herself that she'd thought it. Or very nearly thought it. It had certainly crossed her mind—well, it must have done, mustn't it?—that the description of that fair-haired girl weeping over the pram seemed remarkably reminiscent of Miranda. If only she'd voiced her suspicions then and there, so that now she would have had the right—the duty, almost—to follow up these early speculations! To rush in next door, with all the weight and authority of "I told you so!" behind her, and cast at Norah's shrinking feet all this exciting profusion of supportive evidence!

But, "How do you know?" Norah would immediately and not unreasonably demand; and herein lay the crux of the whole tantalising, infuriating dilemma.

For Janine had promised—had absolutely promised—not to mention to anyone, and particularly not to the Fields themselves, anything of the long and intimate talk she'd had with that dark, intense young woman with the shining loops of black hair and the flashing angry eyes, who'd called on her without warning, quite out of the blue, at crack of dawn.

Well, early, anyway. *Jolly* early. Janine was one of those people who sleep so heavily that waking up in the morning is like recovering from being dead; and so the sound of that front door bell, jangling in her ears at least two hours before she would normally have dreamed of stirring, really did have an impact not unlike the trump of doom.

Still barely conscious, incapable of wondering who the untimely caller could be, she shuffled her feet into her old slippers, and somehow managed to make her way down the stairs.

On first opening the door, still corpse-like with sleep, Janine had very nearly simply shut it again, crept back to bed, pulled the blankets over her ears, and hoped that when she woke next it would all turn out to have been a dream.

For the contrast was just too awful. Here she was, in her early morning death-mask, further embellished by curlers, hairnet, and her All Night Vitamin Anti-Wrinkle Cream, being confronted by this svelte, elegant young woman in a crisp summer dress, spotless sandals, and every hair in place at this unearthly hour. Well, honestly, people have collapsed and died before now at the sight of apparitions far less unnerving: mumbling monks and things, with their heads under their arms, and who disappear anyway at the first grey glimmer of dawn.

But this one didn't disappear. The first grey glimmer of dawn must be long past, the air was already golden and shimmering with the just-risen sun, birds were singing. Before Janine had found the strength to close the door in the face of all that early morning poise and exquisite grooming, the word "Field" seemed to float past the vicinity of her slowly awakening ears. "Miranda Field . . . I wonder if you can by any chance tell me if there's a Miss Miranda Field living around here . . . ?"

Faith moves mountains, they say: and Hope lights up our darkness: but surely the greatest of all is Curiosity? In situations so extreme as to be beyond the reach of either Hope or Faith, there you may still find Curiosity, perky as ever, clinging to the very edge of the abyss. Old men on their death beds have roused up from their comas to demand of their doctor what the hell he thinks he's playing at *now?* Even condemned criminals on the scaffold have sometimes managed to peer sidelong past their blindfold to say, "But why not an ordinary slip knot?"

Nor is this very surprising, for it is to Curiosity that Homo sapiens owes nearly everything he has. Curiosity brought him out of the mud, out of the cave, out of the trammels of a life brutish and short, just as it was now bringing Janine out of the terminal phase of her night's repose, and restoring to her the power of movement and of speech. It was like a shot in the arm. At the words "Miranda Field" the blood began to flow back into her veins, her stiff joints began to stir and flex, and her brain itself started creaking into action under the curlers and the hairnet.

In less than a minute, these impedimenta were no more, and Janine, moribund no longer, was bustling around her kitchen in a bright overall, making coffee for her visitor, and chattering gaily.

If Iris's intention in coming here this morning had been to pick up some bits of information about Miranda's background and antecedents, she must by now have been feeling like a latter-day Sorcerer's Apprentice; or, to bring the parable right up to date, like an easy-going research student who, having chosen as his B.Litt. subject a very minor eighteenth-century poet (one slim volume and a couple of essays), then discovers that the man has also written eighty full-length volumes on the distribution of

Church property in England and Wales between 1740 and 1795, with full appendices on the income therefrom derived.

For the data seemed unstoppable. Miranda Field's pregnancy, her abortion, her kindergarten report, her hamsters, her friendship with the Whittaker girl, her father, her mother, her ne'er-do-well brother who was vaguely supposed to be ill, or something, or maybe it was this rather umpty friend of his who was ill, anyway, no one had set eyes on either of them since they got back from India; and why not?—because neither of them ever got up in the morning, that's why: and as to getting a job, Hell would freeze over before either of those lads stirred a finger in *that* direction.

And the parents? This Mr. and Mrs. Field? Well—between ourselves—between Janine and this total stranger, that is—although Norah Field was such a marvellous person when you got to know her, really *marvellous;* and although Janine wouldn't *dream* of saying one *word* against such a very close friend—nevertheless, in the interests of being *absolutely* frank . . .

The general picture emerged clearly enough. A classic case. Bossy, opinionated mother; loving, ineffectual father, who'd always adored everything about his children except their company. Between Mrs. Field's rigidly permissive principles and Mr. Field's shameless indulgence of every childish whim that looked like being conducive to a few minutes' peace and quiet (such as ice cream off the Tinkabel van in the next road)—between the two of them, though Janine hated to say it of such wonderful, wonderful people, they'd spoiled the kids rotten. And so it was no wonder that this, that, and the other, from the death of Miranda's goldfish on her sixth birthday to Sam's blaring pop music night after night ever since he'd got back from India.

How the conversation moved from all this to the baby-snatching incident, Janine could never afterwards recall.

Throughout the interview, she'd had a vague sense of being "used"; but this feeling, which enrages some women so much, had never bothered Janine at all. After all, what one woman calls "being used" another will call "having fun," and Janine was decidedly among these latter. It seemed to her, when she thought about it at all, that everyone is being "used" all the time, by everyone, from the milkman who'd be out of a job without her late night cup of cocoa and her breakfast cereal, to the greenfly who'd be out of the evolutionary stream altogether if it wasn't for people like her saving enough soft drink labels to send in for Special Bargain Offer Rose Bushes, flower all summer, glorious blooms, crimson/white/yellow please state second choice.

Lucky greenfly! Lucky milkman! And now, lucky Miss Whatsername, seeking to pick Janine's brains about something. This sense of her role as universal provider sometimes quite went to Janine's head, and never more so than now, with this poised and purposeful young woman, obviously well educated, hanging on her every word.

It's nice having your every word hung on, your every opinion noted; but as the conversation—or interview, or whatever you liked to call it—continued, Janine became aware that she was beginning to be just a wee bit indiscreet, or at any rate that it might sound like that if anyone happened to be listening.

But what the hell? Nobody *was* listening; and anyway, what kind of a boring world would it be if everyone was as discreet about everyone else as they all expected everyone else to be about them? Nobody—but absolutely *nobody*—wants you to be discreet about other people, and since there are far more other people than there are of anyone else—and let the statisticians query this if they dare—the sum of human happiness was well served by Janine's philosophy.

It was round about the second brewing-up of coffee, with the sun already hot through the kitchen window, that the subject of the stolen baby came up. It was the visitor who introduced the topic, Janine felt sure, or at any rate it was she who manoeuvred Janine into introducing it. The girl was clever, you had to hand her that. Almost before Janine realised it was happening, there the subject was, being tossed to and fro between them in the most natural manner possible, just as if it had come into the conversation by chance.

It hadn't, though. Janine was herself far too skilled a practitioner at this sort of thing to be deceived.

This, then, was why the young woman was here. This, and this only, was the purpose of her visit: to establish some sort of connection between Miranda Field and the theft of the baby—or, rather, to confirm it, the idea being already clearly established in her mind. All that about having met the Fields on holiday and wanting to look them up again was just so much eyewash.

This girl then, was a policewoman: a plainclothes policewoman on the Snatched Baby case. Yippee! Janine had always longed to be a chief witness in a criminal case. Whenever she read the newspaper reports of criminal trials, she always found herself consumed not with horror, or with pity, or outrage, but with sheer envy of absolutely everyone involved, including the criminal.

And now, here she was, right in the middle of a real live criminal investigation. It was like a dream come true. Then and there she determined to make the most of it, to keep this woman here asking questions for as long as possible, and to give the most intelligent and helpful answers she could, short of actually telling lies. She wanted to make her mark as the most observant and reliable witness they could ever hope to get into the witness box; the judge would commend her clear and precise replies to tricky questions by the Prosecution (or would it be the Defence?) and her picture would be in all the papers. That would make Charlie sit up.

Not that she wished Miranda any harm, of course not;

but it wasn't as if any reticence on Janine's part was going to save her, not at this stage. Clearly, the police already had her marked down as a suspect, or they'd never have sent this policewoman round making enquiries. Probably, it was an open-and-shut case already.

Because, after all, Miranda *had* done it. She must have done. It would be just too much coincidence that a baby should get stolen—and around this neighbourhood, too—just when Miranda had had that abortion, and with her hormones all haywire and everything, the way you read about even after normal childbirth. And then that bit about the fair girl with the pram—and as if all this wasn't enough, just look at her parents! Not that Janine had anything against the Fields, they were her dearest friends, absolute pets, both of them, but all the same, you only had to look at them to know that sooner or later something like this was going to happen. With their heads crammed to the eyebrows with O.K. thoughts, and with their condescending, trendier-than-thou views on absolutely everything, they were just about due for their come-uppance; and this, unmistakably, was it.

She didn't, of course, reveal all this to her interlocutor in so many words—well, she wasn't a common sneak, was she?—but she did cooperate very fully over the enquiries—well, you have to, don't you, when it's the police?—until, after a while, the distinction between cooperation and being a common sneak became more and more blurred, even in her own mind.

It was the heat, partly. Fiercer and fiercer grew the sun through the kitchen window as the morning advanced. First the melting butter, then the curdling bottle of milk had to be hurried into the fridge the other side of the room, and Iris took advantage of one of these forays to get to her feet and suggest, very tentatively and politely, that it might be cooler "in your lovely garden"?

It wasn't lovely: not any more. Janine had never realised, until after Charlie's intemperate departure that

Saturday afternoon without even mowing the lawn, just how much there was to do in the damned plot, and to keep on doing. She'd mowed the lawn herself, almost immediately, just to show him; and then she'd mowed it again, twice; but you'd never know it now, it was a bloody jungle, all over again. And the broad beans had contracted root rot, or leaf blight, or some such disgusting malady; anyway, they'd curled up and died, and so had the spinach seedlings. The lettuce had bolted, the tomatoes wouldn't ripen, and any time Janine, in a sudden burst of vague plans, embarked on any digging, the stinging nettles got there first, leaping in when her back was turned like a cat into the most comfortable armchair.

So, really, there wasn't much to show a visitor and Janine only undertook the tour reluctantly, at the girl's own insistence. Had the guest been anything less than a policewoman, she would have refused point blank, manners or no manners.

Apart from anything else, it was so boring.

"No, those blue things were here when we came, I think," she'd find herself saying; or, "Well, I wouldn't know, I suppose they might be weeds . . ."

It couldn't have been exactly scintillating for the visitor, either; but then (Janine reflected) the police must expect to be bored some of the time in the execution of their duty. They can't always be chasing murderers and things, and falling over precipices in burning cars. And anyway, the woman had brought it on herself; she'd *asked* to be shown round.

Iris was courtesy itself during this tour of inspection, remarking not at all on the neglect and disorder everywhere in evidence, but just chatting pleasantly about the loveliness of the day and the freshness of the air out here in the suburbs. There was only one bad moment; and this was when the visitor—quite without warning—stepped up to the wooden dividing fence and looked over into the next-door garden.

It was awful when anyone did this: really quite shaming, because the Fields, despite all their Meetings and Causes and Progressive hoo-ha's, nevertheless kept their garden immaculate, a showplace, almost. It seemed out of character for such people, Janine thought; and against their principles, too; very un-Have-Not.

Happily, it was looking decidedly less than its best today—no doubt the Fields had plenty of worries on their minds just now—and in addition to this, Janine noted out of the corner of her eye that her companion was not surveying the well-established lawn—such a contrast to Janine's—nor the colourful herbaceous borders, but had her eyes fixed on the one and only eyesore in the whole goddam paradise: the compost heap in the far corner under the great copper beech, where the earth was dark and dank from lack of sun, and nothing would grow, not even ferns.

Luckily, Iris did not stay long enough to have to be offered a drink. The gin was getting a bit low, and after that last letter from Charlie's solicitors, Janine felt a bit uncomfortable about ordering too much more too soon.

She saw Iris off at the front gate, and, as the car moved off down the road, stood there a little longer, scribbling down on a scrap of paper, just for kicks, its registration number and a note of its make and colour.

And so when, later, it was found parked in this same road a little further down, there was no problem at all about identifying it.

CHAPTER 20

There was still quite a bit of the morning left, but Janine found it impossible to settle to anything. The thought of dropping in on Norah still nagged at her intolerably.

She'd *promised* not to say anything; and a promise is a promise, particularly when made to a policewoman. Breaking your word to such a personage might well turn out to be Contempt of Court, or an Infringement of the Official Secrets Act, or something similarly inscrutable and forbidding. And also, greatly though Janine was looking forward to further happenings next door, as many and as dramatic as possible, she naturally didn't want any of them to be her fault. After all, Norah *was* her best friend.

How frustrating it all was! These hoped-for happenings might actually *be* happening, right now, this very moment, and she not know it! That plainclothes woman might have doubled right back, parked her car at the other end of the road, and even now be interviewing poor Norah Field about her daughter's whereabouts. A few mumbled words about "Staying with friends in Derbyshire" might have been good enough for a mere lifelong friend like Janine, but they wouldn't be good enough for the police. "Derbyshire" indeed! Whereabouts in Derbyshire? . . . They'd soon sort *that* one out, with their computers and walkie-talkies and everything.

Poor Norah! Perhaps I *ought* to go in, Janine found herself thinking, just to *warn* her? Without breaking any promises, just to drop here a teeny, teeny hint . . . ?

Teeny hint after teeny hint raced through Janine's

mind in quick succession, and equally quickly had to be discarded for this or that reason: and at last, after biting ragged all of her ten finger nails, she came to her decision. She would just simply call on Norah in a perfectly ordinary way for a perfectly ordinary chat, just as she'd done a million times before. No hints, no leading questions, just a *chat*, for God's sake! Why make such a moral issue of it, such a wrestling with her conscience? Just as if the thing she was about to embark on was a journey into the Dark Night of the Soul?

Damn! Hell and damnation! Norah's back door was locked! This meant that she must be out for the whole day, or even away; she didn't lock up like this just for popping down to the shops. Janine pushed at the door again, hoping that it was maybe just stuck; but no, it was locked all right, and bolted. Standing there, it occurred to Janine that she hadn't in fact seen anything of her neighbour this last couple of days, not even in and out of the garden this lovely weather.

Clearly, it was the duty of a friend to check that all was well.

Back home, Janine rummaged in her kitchen drawer for Norah's front door key. She and Norah had long been in possession of each other's keys as a reciprocal precaution against getting locked out, or some other emergency. Classifying this present situation (perhaps somewhat loosely) as the latter, Janine hurried over with the key, and soon she was standing in the Fields's front hall looking warily around her.

What she had expected to discover by thus gaining entry to her neighbour's home, Janine could not have said. She was to explain it, later, as a "feeling in her bones" that something was wrong; but at the time, if the truth must be told, her bones were feeling pretty ordinary. Only her heart was beating rather faster than normal from the small fear lest someone might suddenly pop out of one of the rooms and ask her what she was doing.

But they didn't; and really it was just as well, because she didn't as yet *know* what she was doing. She just had this feeling that if she poked around a bit, she would sooner or later come upon something which would reveal to her that *this* was what she had come for. There was no knowing in advance what sort of thing it would be, and it was partly this that made the whole escapade so exciting.

The house was very quiet: and it looked neglected, somehow. A film of dust was on the hall table, the flowers in Norah's favourite Doulton vase were withered and drooping. On the ledge—also dusty—were a little pile of letters, and Janine stepped closer, with the intention of examining the postmarks. Not that they told you much these days—a couple of days this way or that on a first-class letter meant nothing, but all the same . . .

Funny, this one! An airmail letter from India, posted in Calcutta less than a week ago, and addressed—so far as Janine could judge—in Sam's own slapdash handwriting.

Funny!—because Sam had been back home several days now, and even if he'd travelled by air—which he hadn't, because the trip was an overland one both ways—it would scarcely have been possible . . .

A slight noise behind her made her whirl round: and it would have been hard to guess, just by looking at them, whether it was she or Edwin Field, rightful owner of the house, who was the intruder: so guilty did they both look; so unmistakably caught-in-the-act.

Someone, sooner or later, had to say something; and since it didn't seem as if it was going to be Edwin, it had to be Janine. With the telltale letter still clutched in her hand, there was no way of dissembling what she'd been at, and so making the best of a bad job, she held it out to him boldly:

"A letter for you both from Sam," she announced

brightly, "Norah'll be pleased, won't she? I know how she worries about him when he doesn't write, the naughty boy!"

Just the right casual, slightly humourous tone, with just the right degree of diversionary content, drawing attention away from her own impertinent prying, and onto the letter itself. "Here!"—she almost thrust it upon the rightful addressee—"he's got as far as Calcutta by the look of it, and I wouldn't be surprised if . . ."

Thus she rattled on in an effort to fill the embarrassing moment with enough, but not too many, appropriate fibs. After all, Edwin Field couldn't *know* that she knew perfectly well that Sam was back home: indeed, he might even assume that she didn't, men being so abysmally ignorant of the tacit to-ings and fro-ings of female communication. Charlie had been the same. "But how do you *know?*" he would pettishly demand of some amusing little anecdote about the neighbour who had taken to keeping her earnings from her part-time job nailed down under the kitchen lino: and always it stopped Janine cold, in mid-story. Anyone who can ask such a question just isn't the sort of person who is capable of understanding the answer.

Preoccupied as she was with reflections such as these, as well as with the necessity for carrying off the present awkward situation as gracefully as possible, it was several seconds before Janine noticed how strangely Edwin Field was behaving. Instead of reaching out gratefully for the letter that she was pressing on him, he was positively backing away from it, with a look of terror in his eyes.

She wasn't to know, of course, that this was his normal reaction to any sort of missive from his son these days. A request for money, it would be; or trouble about some document to which he had, or hadn't, appended his parental signature. Trouble, anyway: that was for sure.

"Yes . . . well . . . thank you," he babbled, moving

back and back from the danger zone as he spoke. "Norah . . . when she comes in . . . Norah will . . ."

Whatever it was, Norah would filter out the bad bits for him and present him with something tidied up and tolerable, as she always had.

After Edwin Field's wary and back-stepping withdrawal into the room from which he had so briefly emerged, Janine stood for a few moments looking after him.

Something was up, that was plain. She'd suspected it all along, and now she was sure.

The possibility that nothing was up, and that this sort of strategic retreat was simply part of Mr. Field's chosen life style, never crossed her mind. Keeping his big foot out of things had never been one of Charlie's failings—she often wished it had—and so it was not one which sprang readily to mind when assessing the husbands of her friends.

Once again, the house seemed very quiet. Whatever it was that its master was occupying himself with behind the closed door of his study, it wasn't making any noise. Janine bestirred herself to lay the Calcutta letter back among the rest, and then stood, hesitating, uncertain where to go from here? The more she thought about it, the more peculiar it seemed about that letter. It *was* Sam's handwriting, she felt sure of it, and yet how could it be, from all that way away, and so recently posted? The most obvious way of satisfying her curiosity, of course, would be to go up right now to that attic flat of Sam's, to knock on the door and *ask* him about the letter, and about his mother's whereabouts and everything. He might accuse her of being nosey, but so what? The young, having no manners themselves, cannot reasonably expect any of their elders—and anyway, what about all that pop music at all hours of the night? That was a splendid card to have up her sleeve—she could, indeed, pretend that that was what she'd come for, to complain that it kept her awake. It didn't, but only because nothing did, which was no thanks to Sam and his friends.

Janine looked at her watch. Nearly lunch time. Surely the young men would be awake by now, even at their age? Indeed, she'd fancied only a moment ago that she'd heard some sort of murmur of sound from the upper floor. Not voices, exactly, but a sort of stirring of activity . . . Already, she had one foot on the lower stair, about to ascend, when she was struck, just in time, by a disagreeable thought.

The hepatitis! That tedious friend of Sam's whose drinking vessels had to be swilled out with boiling water every time he used them—if she ventured up there, she'd be as likely as not to encounter *him* as well as Sam—indeed, it might be he who would answer the door to her, and *that* would be a fine state of affairs, and no mistake! That's all she needed, a slap-up dose of hepatitis, on top of Charlie, and the solicitors' letters, and everything!

Hurriedly, she retreated back into the hall, and after a perfunctory glance into kitchen and sitting room to make sure Norah wasn't around, she beat a hasty retreat out through the front door, breathing in the fresh air in great gulps, and congratulating herself on her escape. What a mercy she'd remembered in time! Why, she might easily have encountered Sam and his plague-ridden friend on the stairs, or anywhere, because there was no doubt, now, that they were up and about. Already those first murmurs of awakening life had escalated to full-blown pop music, blaring impudently from those top-floor windows and seeming to follow her down the garden path deliberately, like a rude noise.

CHAPTER 21

The sleeping pills Tim had given her last night seemed to be affecting Miranda still. All day she'd been drifting in and out of sleep, aware all the time of deep misery, but incapable of sustained thinking about it. Perhaps he had intended just this; or perhaps, totally unaccustomed as she was to this kind of drug, a very moderate dose could have had this effect on her. How much he'd given her, she had no idea, she hadn't been counting. You don't count any more, or weigh up the things people are doing for you, when you are sunk to this level of grief and guilt and humiliation.

Because he knew. Of course he knew. They all must know by now. Though no one had ventured on an open accusation, or even the mildest of interrogations, the new attitude of withdrawal and of shrinking embarrassment was unmistakable. With relief they'd taken her word for it that she'd "rather be alone": thankfully they'd tiptoed away, silently, like a retreating army, under cover of darkness. She'd heard them moving furtively around the flat, whispering to one another, as wary of disturbing her as if she'd been planted here by terrorists. Soon, no doubt, the bomb disposal squad would be on its way; but before she could know whether this was to be the case or not, she had been pushed by the sleeping pills down, down into impenetrable oblivion.

Miranda was wrong, actually, in assuming that they *all* knew of her disgrace. Alison, Belinda, and Merve were still taking the situation at its face value, and innocently assuming that what their companion was suffering from was simple grief at losing her baby. Had she known this, she might have found it easier to rouse herself and speak to them when, one by one, they peered into her room next morning before leaving for work, and then tiptoed silently away.

But she could not have known, for she had hitherto had no experience of people's reactions to grief, and the extent to which these can be almost indistinguishable from their reactions to the most heinous crime. Either way, the victim becomes for the time being an outcast, mercilessly debarred from normal society and its cheerful, healing interchanges.

Merciless in effect, that is: not merciless in intention, not at all. The trouble is, that there *is* no way of treating a grief-stricken person normally. To try to do so is like trying to play tennis with someone who has lost his racket and can't return the balls. No matter how sympathetic you are, or how fully you understand his longing—his desperate need, even—for an ordinary, straight-forward game such as you used to enjoy together, it is impossible to give it to him. Normality is a two-way thing, and not all the compassion and understanding in the world can cancel out that fact.

And thus it was that Alison and Belinda, full of sorrow and sympathy as they undoubtedly were, could still only creep around, embarrassed and furtive, exactly as they would have done had they known all about their friend's guilty secret and were condemning her out of hand.

Only Merve, typing away as if nothing had happened, was unwittingly offering a crumb of comfort. As she dozed and woke, and dozed and woke again through the long day, it was dimly reassuring to hear the steady tap-tap-tap of something going on in the world which had nothing at all to do with her. For it is down there, in the very depths of despair, that one comes at last upon that ultimate, rock-bottom security which in happier times goes unrecognised: the simple fact that one's own feelings are not, after all, co-extensive with the universe, and that for someone, somewhere, something else is going on.

It was a pity that Merve, castigating himself (every now and again) for heartlessness, did not realise that by thus carrying on as usual he was tapping a small message of comfort and reassurance to the grief-stricken victim on the other side of the dividing wall.

There was to be one other brief respite before the long, dreadful day darkened at last into night. Drowsing away the last hours of daylight, Miranda was suddenly shocked awake by a loud, unfamiliar voice, shouting, it almost seemed, right into her ear:

"There's somebody in *my* bed!" it bellowed, like all the Three Bears rolled into one, and Miranda found herself staring into a large, sallow face surrounded by a mass of frizzy hair. "Who the hell . . . ? Look, I do think, *honestly—No,* I did *not* say I was moving in permanently with Keith. Am I crazy?—I wouldn't move in with that rat if I was . . . !"

Christine, of course. It was bound to happen sooner or later, and Miranda could only feel relief that it was happening now. A diversion. A happening. Someone who was furious with her at last, instead of pitying and embarrassed. At least it would bring to an end all this whispering and tiptoeing.

But it didn't. Almost at once, the intruder—or, rather, the rightful owner—was hustled out of the room, and an absolute storm of anxious, explanatory whispering burst upon the evening air.

". . . move her at a time like this . . . !"

". . . well, the settee, then. Look, Chris, surely, just for one night . . . ?"

And then, "Shush, she'll hear!" someone hissed; and someone else softly closed the door. For a few minutes, Miranda could hear nothing more than the faint, electric whirr of charge and countercharge. At one point, someone must have been reminding Christine of the principles on which the Squat was founded, for her voice suddenly rose to shriek:

"That's all bloody fine, but why do *I* always get the grotty end of Peace and Love?" she demanded, perhaps not unreasonably. And then, "Shush!" once again, and the dispute relapsed back into relative inaudibility.

Keith this. Keith that. Teaching a lesson to the bloody little swine . . . Lulled by such soothing evidences of the continued existence of troubles other than her own, Miranda felt herself growing drowsy once more.

But this time, she must fight it. Because now, if ever, was her chance to slip away unnoticed, while they were all in there arguing. She could creep softly along the passage and out through the front door, closing it gently behind her, and disappear forever.

Disappear where? Where would she go? Back to the vast, anonymous air terminal, where all night long you could slump unnoticed, among other slumped figures from every corner of the globe; silent, when necessary, in a dozen languages? It had worked O.K. the first night, with an extended Cypriot family to her right and an even more extended Brazilian family to her left, each assuming that she was one of the uncountable cousins belonging to the other: but the second night had been hazardous in the extreme, and her physical exhaustion well-nigh unendurable. It had seemed to her, this time, that people had their eyes on her, puzzled, suspicious, and more than once, some kindly official or other had paused to question her. Was she on her own? Waiting for friends, then? Did she need any help? Was she sure she was all right? It was a policewoman this time, with a huge moon-face and frizzy hair just like Christine's, leaning over her, grinning like a wolf, all teeth and glistening tongue, and hissing, "We know who you are . . . it's no use lying! We have found you out . . . !"

Miranda's scream of terror made no sound; her limbs, as she tried to leap up from the bench and run, seemed to be paralysed; and she woke, sweating, and gasping for breath, to find that it was already night. The little airless room was now quite dark. The tiptoeing and whispering had ceased. It must be pretty late. Even Merve's typewriter had fallen silent, which rarely happened before one or two in the morning. Unless, of course, he was having Writers' Block again.

Yes, that must be it. For the silence was not quite like an ordinary silence, it was shot through with the sense of someone being wide awake; alert and expectant, waiting . . .

Waiting for what? Struggling out of her nightmare, Miranda had had the feeling of having been woken by some sound, some movement? But as the silence continued, thick and unbroken, the sensation faded, and she was able to persuade herself that it was simply the nightmare itself that had roused her, as nightmares do. Gradually, the beating of her heart slowed down, and her breathing returned to normal.

But the sense of being not the only one awake in this silent house still clung about her: and somehow it wasn't a companionable feeling, not at all. Rather, it was a feeling of being under observation.

And only gradually, over several minutes, did these vague sensations of unease begin to crystallise into something real and tangible.

She *was* under observation. There was someone in the room, right now, close by the bed, sitting absolutely still, and breathing so softly, so carefully, that the indrawn air was indistinguishable from the faint stirrings of the night air through the half-open window.

Christine, was it? Was the irate newcomer plotting some kind of silent takeover of her rights, now that the rest of them were safely asleep? *Was* she? The Christine of the loud voice, the pile of tatty footwear? It didn't seem like her, somehow.

And, indeed, it wasn't her.

"You're awake, aren't you Miranda?" came Iris's voice softly out of the darkness. "You've been awake some time, haven't you, planning how to get away? Only you don't dare!"

For a moment, Miranda felt herself in the presence of witchcraft, so accurately did the cool, disembodied voice describe her state of mind. It was as if Iris had all this time been creeping around the inside of her skull, making notes of what she found.

Silly! It didn't actually need second sight to envisage the turmoil of fear and despair into which the events of the last few days would have thrown her! With the darkness between them like some great, soft barrier, Miranda strove to frame an answer.

"Of course I'm going away," she began huskily. "Obviously, I can't stay here any more, now that . . ."

"Obviously you can't"—Iris picked up the phrase with bitter glee—"and you're not going to be allowed to, either, so don't worry! But you're not just quitting the scene of the crime scot free, if that's what you had in mind! *Oh*, no. You're going to pay the penalty for what you've done. You're going to pay, and pay, and pay . . ."

What I've done . . . She's right. I've done a terrible thing. She's known all along—and now the rest of them know, too. But do they know *everything*? How can they? How can even *she* know that . . . ?

Leaning closer, as though to catch the last words of a dying friend, Iris set herself to answer each of these unspoken questions exactly as if she had heard them, dealing with each one systematically, and very, very softly.

"Of course, I knew from the start that you weren't really pregnant, you were only pretending. It was just too obvious for words, if you don't mind my saying so! And now Tim knows, too. Yes, I told him. Well, of course I did, I had to, it was only right that he should know. He could hardly believe it at first, but now—Oh, Miranda, I wish you could have seen his face! So disgusted . . . ! So disillusioned . . . !"

The fact that this disgust, this disillusion, were mainly directed against herself, Iris did not see fit to reveal, for the injustice of it was almost beyond endurance.

"Watching the poor kid like a cat watching a mouse," he'd accused; and, by God, this night he was going to learn more about cats than he'd ever dreamed of; and about mice, too, and about the distinguishing marks by which you can tell which is which . . .

In the terrible darkness she gave a low laugh.

"He was so appalled, poor man, he could hardly bring himself to say your name! But it doesn't matter, does it, dear, because after this you'll never see him again—" And then, after a tiny pause, "They won't let you."

They? Who was "they"? Momentarily startled out of her silent despair Miranda struggled to frame her question, but in that instant, and completely without warning, Iris switched on the bedside light. For just one second Miranda's white, shamed face was revealed, blinking helplessly under the pitiless illumination; then, with a swift, small convulsion of her whole body, she twisted out of sight under the bedclothes, only her humped shoulders marking the spot.

Iris waited, quietly and without impatience, for what she knew must happen next; and sure enough, presently, muffled under layer upon layer of blankets, there came a voice as from the Confessional, babbling forth its crimes and its muddled penitence.

"I—I'm sorry, Iris! Deceiving you all like that—it was horrible—dreadful! I just can't tell you how terribly terribly sorry I am. I mean, it was *awful* of me, I know it was, but somehow there seemed to be no way out—can you understand? I mean, with all of you being so kind, and taking me in specially *because* I was pregnant—and—you know! The things Tim said—and him being so sweet to me, and so concerned—and the knitting, and everything; how *could* I tell her when she'd already begun decreasing for the *neck* . . . ! Oh, Iris, I didn't know *what* to do, and the nicer you all were to me the worse it got! And then, you know"—here the humped blankets shuddered in the circle of light, and a low choking sound came from deep within, the rumblings of uncontrollable sobbing—"you know, Iris, I'd been *so* unhappy! Before I ever came here, I mean—at home—so *terribly* unhappy, that's why I ran away. Because I *had* been pregnant, you know, really and truly pregnant, but I—I—lost it! It's so *awful,* when that happens—so dreadfully, impossibly awful, I don't know how to explain! The mad, terrible feelings you get—Oh, Iris, if you only *knew* . . . !"

"I do know, actually," Iris remarked quietly. "I know because I've had those feelings too, exactly the same. I've had an abortion too, you know, just like you have, the only difference being that *I* didn't use it to wreck everything around me; to destroy my family, to betray my friends, to abuse their hospitality. Nor did I regard it as a good and sufficient reason for stealing another woman's baby and murdering it."

A great lurching of bedclothes, a strangled cry. Miranda lunged upwards with staring eyes and gaping mouth.

"I—I—! But, Iris, you *can't* suppose . . . !" was all she'd managed to gasp out before Iris's hand was across her mouth, silencing her.

"Hush! You'll be waking the whole house!" she admonished; and then, as Miranda choked and struggled under the restraining hand: "Yes, my dear, you may well choke on that lie you're trying to tell me! The lie you're planning to tell everyone—Tim too, of course! You're gambling on the likelihood that the poor sap will believe this lie, too, just as he believed the lie about your pregnancy!

Or did, until I put him wise; and I'm going to put him wise this time, too.

"You murdered that baby, Miranda, and I'm going to prove that you did. Prove it to Tim, and perhaps to the police too; that depends on *you,* my dear, somewhat; we'll have to see.

"Anyway, prove it I will, and *you're* going to help me. So up you get, and get yourself dressed. I'd put on something warm if I were you, the night air is treacherous, is it not? Anyway, come along, get a move on, we haven't got all night. We need to get there before the moon sets, of course, and it's quite a distance, as you well know.

"I said, *get up!* Or do you want me to wake Tim and take *him* with me, instead?—see what *he* says when I show him what I've found? How about *that,* eh . . . ?

"Aha! I *thought* that would get you moving! Good girl!"

CHAPTER 22

Iris drove carefully and without obvious haste through the empty moonlit streets, though in fact her mind leapt and churned with the urgency of the task ahead: to be run in for speeding while on such an errand would have been the final irony.

The risk that Miranda might scream and struggle and try to get out when she began to realise whither they were bound, had also been on her mind; but here, it seemed, she'd been overestimating the dangers. Her companion sat limp as a doll in the passenger seat, hands folded and mouth half open. You would have thought she was asleep were it not for her eyes, round, surprised doll's eyes, fixedly staring.

Glancing swiftly sideways, Iris was conscious of a stirring of unease. Had the girl actually gone insane? That hadn't been the idea at all. The insane are not responsible, they escape the consequences of their actions, no matter how frightful these actions may be; they have put themselves beyond the range of ordinary judgement, of blame, of hatred, of revenge. Iris did not wish Miranda to be beyond the range of these, she wanted her to suffer the full impact of them all, deprived, at last, of the uncritical protection of Tim's pity and compassion.

Oh, that compassion of his!—that idiot tolerance, gushing inexhaustibly, as from a broken main. Right now, Iris could almost hear his voice, his special, holier-than-thou voice that he kept for talking about Miranda: "But Iris, the poor kid didn't know what she was doing . . . she's been having some kind of a breakdown . . . the strain . . . the unhappiness . . . can't you understand? . . . have you no compassion . . . ?"

"The poor kid . . . !" If she heard that phrase from his lips just once more, she'd . . . he'd . . .

Watch it, Iris, watch it! A red light is a red light even at three in the morning, and no other car in sight for miles. She dare not—simply *dare* not—risk tangling with the police tonight for however trivial an offence. Fuming, swallowing her sense of urgency like a great plum stone, almost choking on it, Iris braked, and set herself to live through the long seconds before the lights should change.

She stole another quick glance at her companion. Please God, let her not be actually, clinically mad: that will ruin everything.

Whether God indeed answers prayers of such pure and undiluted hatred must be open to doubt; but anyway, whether in answer to her prayer or by mere coincidence, Iris found her fears almost at once set at rest by a small frightened voice—yes, frightened, not mad—addressing her out of the semi-darkness:

"Where . . . where are you taking me, Iris? Where are we supposed to be going . . . ?"

Not mad, no: but bloody silly. Did the girl not realise, even now, what was going to happen to her? Did she not understand that Iris, by now, knew everything?

"You stole another woman's baby and murdered it," Iris had accused her, in so many words, less than an hour ago. It could hardly be put plainer than that.

Was the girl stupid, had she not taken it in properly? Or was she, rather, cunning, imagining that even at this late stage she might still bluff her way out of it with her innocent-young-girl act which had gone down so big with Tim once—and indeed might do so again if Iris didn't play her cards carefully . . . ?

Or was she gambling on the possibility that Iris might

have been only guessing, making a shot in the dark in the hope of startling a confession out of her victim?

Because, of course, Miranda couldn't know—for Iris hadn't yet told her—how damning was the evidence against her; nor what it was that Iris had seen with her own eyes, had almost—but not quite—actually touched with her pink, well-manicured finger tips.

"Where . . . where are we going, Iris?" came the small voice again—and either the girl really was quite bewildered and baffled, or else she was a consummate actress.

Well, and she was, wasn't she? She'd been acting nonstop for weeks, and well enough to fox the lot of them—except, of course, for Iris herself.

Not that it mattered. Super-cunning or plain stupid, there was no need for a straight answer.

"You'll see soon enough," Iris said, between clenched teeth; and then, unable to stop there, she continued: "You know, don't you, that this is where the play-acting is going to stop? Your days of deceit and pretence and sham innocence are over, my dear, as will soon be clear to you. I told you I had proof of what you've done, didn't I?—and I have. We are going to look at it together. And later on, Tim is going to look at it, too. He is going to know you at last for what you are—an evil, treacherous, cold-blooded little murderer! That goddam compassion of his is going to take some knocks tonight, I promise you, and so is that interminable idiot tolerance. 'You've no proof!' he shouted at me—and, by God, if it's proof he wants, it's proof he's going to get, shoved right into his arms, worms and all . . . !"

Proof! Tim had laughed at her, contemptuously, when she'd flung the word at him yesterday evening. "Spite" he'd called it. "Pure spite! You've always had it in for the poor kid! You *can't* have any proof, it's ridiculous! Murder, indeed! Well, go on then, *give* me some proof! Just give me some!"

Shush, Tim, stop shouting, no need to wake the whole house. You want proof? You shall have proof—and from her own lying little lips at that . . .

"Don't you dare . . . !" He was shouting again, and Iris had to shush him once more. In a low, bitter whisper he repeated the words: "Don't you dare! You're not to say one word to the poor kid about your filthy suspicions! Do you understand? Not one word! As her medical adviser, I forbid it! She is not to be worried about anything, not anything at all, in her present state . . ."

Well, tough: that had been the substance of Iris's reply; and she'd gone on to point out that Lizzie Borden (if her memory served her) was trying to calm her nerves with a nice cup of tea when they came for her.

"Like I say, tough. That's the trouble with committing murder."

"What do you mean, Iris?" came the small voice again. "You can't really think that I—"

The little fool! Could she really be supposing that all this damn-fool innocence was going to get her anywhere?

And the awful thing was, that it might! Look at the lies Tim had swallowed already?—what was to stop him swallowing more? He seemed to thrive on the diet . . .

"Look," she said, "you aren't going to get away with it, do you know that? Yes, I know that Tim, poor sap, will try to believe you in the teeth of all the evidence—but don't kid yourself it's for the sake of your blue eyes! It isn't; it's for his own sake, and for the sake of his bloody career! Well, think about it; what sort of start will it be to a newly qualified young doctor's career to have been harbouring under his roof a psychopathic murderer? Either knowingly, which makes him a criminal, or unknowingly, which makes him a fool? Who's going to want a fool for a doctor? Or a criminal either? His career will be finished before it's begun. What Hospital Management Board do you think is going to employ him after seeing his picture plastered over the front page of every newspaper in the land alongside this blond murderess!—and under-age with it . . . !

"Or did you think, dear, that he was all set to sacrifice All for Love? My God—Tim doesn't sacrifice things for *love*—didn't you know? *I* could have told you—but you didn't ask, did you?

"Well, there you are. That's it. The party's over. *This* time, I have evidence that is overwhelming, incontrovertible . . . and you and I, together, are going to unearth it . . ."

She gave a sudden, wild laugh: "'Unearth'—that's good, isn't it! . . . Really rich . . . ! Don't you think so?"

She shot a swift, sidelong glance at the white, quivering face, and laughed again, more softly.

"Yes, you may well shiver and shake, Miranda! You're in a state of shock, aren't you? That's what Tim tells me, did you know? 'She's in a state of shock,' he says, all grave and professional: I just couldn't stop giggling!

"Don't misunderstand me, my dear. I'm not questioning his diagnosis. Oh dear no, as if I would! I'm sure you *are* in a state of shock, anyone would be after committing so obscene and horrible a crime! I wouldn't be surprised, you know"—this in gentle, reassuring tones—"if lots of murderers don't feel just the way you do. I expect, if we only knew, they're in a dreadful state of nerves for days afterwards: can't sleep: can't eat: the lot. Nightmares, too, I wouldn't be surprised.

"Which reminds me, what *was* that nightmare you were having just before you woke? You were cheeping and twitching like a new-born kitten, and so I knew that inside your head you were screaming at the top of your voice. You were, weren't you? Screaming . . . screaming . . . and running away . . . running, running, running! Away from what, I wonder? I'd just love to know!"

Still Miranda did not answer. Not that it mattered. Iris felt that she knew by heart, already, all the lies that were still to fall from those tremulous, half-open lips. Lies about where she'd been hiding during those two days of her absence; lies about those telephone calls announcing the birth of Baby Caroline.

"I . . . I just *couldn't* say that she was *dead!* I just couldn't make myself say the words!" Miranda had already stammered in answer to an earlier query of Iris's as to why, if she wanted to keep up the farce of having been pregnant, she hadn't simply rung up to say that the baby had been born dead? Surely that was the obvious way out of the dilemma?

"Oh, I know, Iris, I *know,* and that's exactly what I'd planned to do . . . that's exactly what I kept *trying* to do! I kept nerving myself to do it, but there were those great queues for the telephones at the air terminal, and so by the time I got there, I found I'd lost my nerve, and I just couldn't say it . . . To say aloud, in words, that Baby Caroline was dead—I just couldn't—I felt it was actually *making* her be dead—it felt like killing her, all over again! And so I kept putting it off—kept saying she was alive, just one more time . . . *Next* time, I kept telling myself, I'll tell them she's dead . . . but I still couldn't! To actually say it . . . Oh, Iris, can't you understand . . . ?"

A likely story! Just *how* likely, given all the circumstances, Iris was in no mood to notice, for she had already made up her mind that whatever Miranda told her in the course of the journey would necessarily be lies.

But the *end* of the journey—Ah, that would be another matter! There, at the end of this moonlit ride, was the place where the lying had to stop. Under the great, damp, overhanging trees, where only the faint, occasional moonbeam flickered upon the dark, fallen leaves below . . .

What would Miranda's defence be *then,* as she stood upon the very spot, confronting the evidence with her own eyes, touching it with her own hands? And when they took the thing home and laid it in Tim's arms, all streaked with fresh earth and with dead leaves clinging to it here and there, then what would *he* say? . . . How would he defend his precious protégé *then* . . . ?

Out of her mind. Maybe this was where you had to be in order to understand that place beyond the mind; that region from which the rational intellect shrinks back affrighted, and where the tortured soul runs free.

Iris understood that place all too well; she knew those dark, terrible regions like the back of her hand; had even, as best she could, tried to describe them to Tim, but what was the use, when he was only a man, and such a young one at that? How could *he* understand the crippling jealously, the blinding, uncontrollable rage against every smug, contented young mother pushing a healthy rosy baby in front of her, as in a Roman triumph, through the suburban streets? A baby whom she has been allowed to bring to full term, to bear, to enjoy, to show off in all its glory? How could Tim, or any man, be expected to understand the intensity of that rage, that envy? Or comprehend the mad longing, born of despair and grief, to destroy, destroy, destroy . . . to wipe forever from those fulfilled, maternal faces, the smugness and the joy . . .

Oh, and the *effort* it required, the mighty, almost superhuman exercise of will power, to keep these awful impulses in check; to control them, to batten them down, day after day, week after week, along every pram-strewn street, in and out of every shop, until gradually, they began to lose their demonic power.

How could anyone understand it, who had only ever been a man?

But Iris understood it. Oh yes, Iris could comprehend the hugeness of the temptation by which Miranda had been overwhelmed; and at the very core of her hatred and black fury against the girl, there was a strange sense of comradeship, on some level too deep to explore, or even acknowledge; a sense of having been through fire and water together; and if Miranda had succumbed to the awful pressures, while Iris had resisted them, it seemed, in these black, subterranean regions of the mind, to be almost a trivial difference . . .

But when Iris had tried to explain all this to Tim, revealing to him for the very first time the fearful, murderous impulses that had been triggered off by her own abortion; confiding in him secrets of her soul that she'd never dreamed of confiding before—what had he done?

He'd turned on her, that's what. Turned on her in fury —a very young man's fury, compounded of guilt, fear, and sheer dismay.

So she was dragging all *that* up again, was she? Was she *never* going to let it rest? Was she going to pursue him, like the Furies after Orestes, tormenting him for the rest of his life, never forgiving, never forgetting, hell-bent on making him pay, and pay, and pay, for that one small slip? Hell, he'd *said* he was sorry, hadn't he? He'd done what he could to help her through it—helped her with the arrangements, the money . . . what more could a man do? And it had been *her* idea, anyway, the whole bloody mess-up, *he'd* never pushed her into the damned abortion, never pressured her . . . And as for bringing it up again *now,* all these months later, and dragging that poor kid into it as a stick to beat him with . . . !

"That poor kid." He'd said it just once too often. Just like she'd known he would.

They were through central London now, and into the further suburbs, cruising through quiet, tree-lined streets; detached houses with neat lawns in front of them, and tall shrubs throwing shadows of inky blackness across the silent, moonlit road.

"Recognise where we are now?" Iris remarked nonchalantly, with barely a glance at her companion: but Miranda made no answer. Only her eyes grew wider and wider, with incredulous terror, as they coasted quietly onwards, through ever more and more familiar streets, towards their destination.

CHAPTER 23

Iris was careful to park at the far end of the road in order not to attract the attention of any nearby neighbours who might, for one reason or another, be peering out of their darkened bedroom windows at this dead hour. Probably none were, but you couldn't be too careful.

It was a windless night, and in the well-kept front gardens on either side of the road not a leaf stirred. There was no need, any longer, to urge Miranda to be silent; her fear of drawing attention to herself, in this place, at this hour, was by now as great as Iris's own. Only when they came to a halt outside one of the dark houses looming against the moon-washed sky, did Miranda's sharp intake of breath make a tiny whiplash of sound on the still air. Her lips formed, silently, the words "No! No!" as Iris's hand reached towards the latch of the front gate; but she dared take her protest no further. Meek as a shadow, she followed Iris across the square of lawn, past the familiar display of late summer flowers—dahlias, hollyhocks, geraniums, all grey together under the moon—and into the shadows beyond.

The side gate was unlocked, as always. Neither Mr. nor Mrs. Field believed very much in burglars; the long years of referring to them as "Victims of Society" had blunted their sense of the reality of these beings; and so far, they'd been lucky. Or was it, perhaps, that burglars, just as much as ghosts, tend to manifest themselves to believers rather than to sceptics? To be treated as if you don't exist is no boost to any ego, supernatural or otherwise, and it may well be that burglars actually *need* a few barred windows, the odd mortice lock, to give them a sense of identity, and hence the courage to pursue their calling.

Be that as it may, the side gate was not only unlocked, it was ajar, and so the two intruders—for thus Miranda, too, felt herself to be—were enabled to slip through without so much as the creak of a hinge.

The side entrance between the two tall houses was dark as any dungeon, very narrow, and lit only by a tiny strip of night sky far above. Iris, fearful of stumbling, inched her way along, hands outstretched against unpredictable obstacles. Miranda, of course, had no need of such precautions; without even thinking, she knew exactly where the dustbins were, and the bundle of raspberry canes, and the disused water butt, and the sacks of peat, of fertiliser, and the special stuff for the tomatoes . . .

The light of the full moon, when they emerged from the dark passage into the back garden, was almost blinding. Miranda caught her breath. It was as if she was seeing the garden for the first time—her own garden, whose every stone, every contour was as familiar to her as her own body. Here she had played as far back as she could remember; had worked, and read, and built tree-houses; had dawdled away long summer afternoons dreaming, giggling, writing poetry, growing from babyhood to girlhood under the shade of those grand trees, or sprawled out in the sunshine on that smooth, spacious lawn that now lay before her like a silver sea, lapping to her very feet. Had she never, in all these years, seen the garden under a full moon before, that it should look so strange to her now, so magical, like a garden in a dream? And as they moved forward softly, inexorably, across that expanse of shining grass, it was like paddling in a sea of light.

But the grass was somehow not quite what her feet had

been expecting. It was longer than usual . . . rough . . . uncared-for; and as the soles of her feet registered this small change, she experienced a stab of such grief, such shock, as was quite beyond her comprehension. She gave, involuntarily, a tiny gasp of surprise and dismay . . . and immediately felt Iris's hand on her shoulder, hard.

"Quiet!" whispered the older girl, peremptorily; or, rather, formed the words silently with her lips, grey as the grass in this unearthly light; and Miranda, tense with unimaginable dread and foreboding, obeyed.

On, on they went, across the silver, dew-soaked grass, until at last they waded out of the light and into the darkness cast by the great trees at the end of the garden.

Here, under the spreading branches, where the sun never reached, it was already autumn. The tang of dead leaves from the compost heap was in Miranda's nostrils—and another smell, too—fungus was it, or the damp, lichened bark of the great copper beech which filled half the sky, breaking up the moonlight into tiny slivers of uncertain light, scattered here and there on the dark earth like dropped silver coins? Beneath her feet, the soil was dank and lumpy, as if recently dug over; and a little way ahead the wavering pillar of darkness that was Iris came to a halt. In the flickering shreds of moonlight she, too, could have been a tree, rooted in its chosen spot, motionless.

"Here!" breathed Iris, beckoning, and speaking in a voice no louder than the stir of a snake gliding through tall grass towards its prey. "Here, where I'm standing . . . No, not *that* way, you little fool! *This* way! As if you didn't know . . . ! Ah, that's better; that's more like it! But nearer, please. Nearer . . . !"

Miranda, shuddering from head to foot with a terror and revulsion for which she could find no words, tried to obey, for she knew in her bones, now, that there could be no escape. The moonlit garden was a dream garden no longer, but a nightmare from which she was never going to wake; and as she took one more dragging, reluctant step forward, she seemed to feel the horror emanating from the very soil beneath her feet . . . and now Iris's hand was on her arm again, vise-like, and her voice, thick with hatred, issued its final warning:

"*Tim!*" it whispered, "if you're scared, then I'll bring Tim here instead, and *he* can help me! How about that, eh?"—and at once Miranda, obedient as any robot, moved quickly across the remaining foot or two of space and stood on the required spot, blankly, as if waiting further instructions about the conduct of her own execution.

"Hold out your hand!" whispered Iris, her voice quivering, now, with impending triumph: and as if this was a children's party game, in which some delightful little surprise was about to be popped into her white, upturned palm, Miranda did as she was told.

A trowel it was that she got, sharp-edged and clean, its brand-new blade ever so faintly gleaming in the flickers of moonlight that came and went with the trembling of her hand.

"Dig!" commanded Iris, in a whisper low as ever, and yet somehow shrill through her clenched teeth. "Go on—*dig!* No, not *there*, you little fool—here! *Here!* As if you didn't know! Of course you know, you know the exact, precise spot, even better than I do! So stop fooling and get on with it! Dig, I say! *Dig!*"

Miranda's hand was trembling so much that she could scarcely wield the tool. She tried one last, desperate plea for mercy:

"Oh, Iris . . . ! Oh, please . . . If you'd only *tell* me . . . ! That is . . . I mean . . . !"

"*Tell* you?—Tell you what? There's no need to tell you anything, the answer's right there, under your feet. You just have to dig for it, that's all!

"So *dig*, you little monster! Dig . . . ! Dig . . . !"

And sure enough, as though hypnotised, brain washed, pixilated under the moon, Miranda dug. Dug into the clayey, heavy soil which ordinarily would have been heavy work indeed, but tonight it was light and effortless as a dream, so recently and so thoroughly had it been dug over already, the thick clay broken and loosened.

Down through the surface Miranda dug, the new shiny trowel sliding easily among the newly broken clods; deeper and deeper into the damp soil, the speckles of moonlight moving ever so faintly hither and thither across her work, like the ghosts of little hopping white birds, so that sometimes she could get a glimpse of what she was doing, and sometimes could only wildly and desperately guess.

A whitish gleam against the dark soil . . . a curious muffling obstacle to the next thrust of the trowel . . . something, some alien object, was coming to light. In the faint, uncertain moonbeams it looked, at first, like some monstrous toadstool, greyish, bulbous, and oddly shaped: but toadstools do not have tiny pearl buttons sewn two-and-two across their width; nor do they have grubby nylon ribbon dangling like a long white worm from a filthy gathered neckline.

"Dig! Dig!" The excitement in Iris's voice was almost out of control . . . And now a small knitted sleeve was appearing, gathered at the wrist . . . a vague, whitish tangle of flannelette . . . more pearl buttons . . . and below that . . . what *was* this, bigger than all the rest, and harder to shift? Yes, a pair of knitted leggings, bulging, bulky, difficult to pull free. There was something inside them . . . something heavy, soft, resistant: was it just an accumulation of damp clay and soil that had worked their way inside the garment: or was it . . . ? Was it . . . ?

Miranda's fingers sprang back from that soft, mysterious heaviness as if of their own volition.

For a moment, her throat seemed to close up completely, as if she was going to die.

Then, suddenly, it opened, and the cry that came from

it was the most ancient cry in the world. It is the cry that comes from tiny children waking in a dark room; from soldiers mortally wounded on the battle field; and even from the cracked, ancient lips of old, old women in geriatric wards, so far gone in senility that all other power of speech has left them. When all else has faded from their dying brains, this one word they can still scream out, loud and clear, out of the dark backward of eighty, ninety, or a hundred years ago:

"Mummy! Mummy! Mummy!"

Miss X was jerked wide awake, and at first she could not make out what it was that had roused her. Could it be that damned radio, which she kept on, softly, softly, all the hours of the day and night, so that she could turn up the volume to its ear-splitting maximum at a moment's notice whenever it became necessary?

Was it necessary now? Could this be what it was that had woken her—a sleepy, hiccuppy whimper from the improvised cradle, warning her that it was once again time for a feed, and that a bottle must yet again be hastily, furtively prepared?

She hadn't intended to fall asleep at all, it was too dangerous: but weariness, the utter, bone-piercing weariness of these past days and nights, had once more caught up with her, and she must have dropped off, right here in this straight-backed wooden chair.

Perhaps she'd dreamed the sudden sound? She'd been dreaming *something*, certainly, just before she'd been startled awake, but what it was she could no longer recall. She felt sure, now, that the whole thing had been triggered off by that endlessly muttering radio, yap, yap, yap, just below the threshold of consciousness. Perhaps the barely audible voice had switched suddenly to barely audible pop music, or vice versa, thus recalling to her subconscious . . . ?

Yes! That was it! *That* was what she'd been dreaming

of, and not for the first time, either. It all came back to her now, just as it had been at the very beginning; the bland, reassuring radio voice of that psychiatrist, on the very evening after she'd committed her crime. How wise he'd sounded, how benevolent, how full of understanding! With such sympathy had he described her, Miss X's, predicament, exactly as if he had known her, getting it all magically, exactly right: the aching, desperate need for a new love object to replace the one that had gone; the blank hostility and incomprehension of those nearest and dearest to her; the alienation from the family which had once been close and loving; the sudden, overwhelming trauma, the guilt, the shattering realisation that the person she loved most in the world, the person to whom she had given fifteen years of total, unconditional loyalty and love, and for whose sake she had faced the most difficult, the most painful decision of her whole life—to realise, after all this, that this person was turning upon her not with gratitude, but with hatred, bitterness, and contempt.

"I hate you. I hate you!" had been the parting message, on a torn-off scrap of paper, the sole memento, now, of all those happy years of love and closeness. "I hate you. I hate you!"

She half wished, now, that she'd taken him at his word, that radio psychologist, had given herself up as he'd urged, and had thrown herself on his mercy—or on the mercy of his doubtless equally sympathetic and understanding colleagues. She'd have been dealt with leniently, as he had promised, and he would have helped her, sustained her, lavished upon her all the sympathy and wisdom of his calling: well, of course he would, for was not her case the exact replica of the one he'd been describing with such compassion and understanding?

An exact replica, that is, except in just one all-important, and wholly damning, respect. Because throughout his whole talk, in all its wisdom and tolerance, he'd been labouring under an awful misapprehension; he'd been assuming, all along, that the unhappy perpetrator of this "crime of love" (as he called it) was someone *young*, and therefore entitled to feelings of loss, and abandonment, and desperate longing for love. In an older woman, like Miss X, a middle-aged mother of teenage children, these exact same feelings are called possessiveness.

From the improvised cardboard box cradle, there came a small whimper, a stir of awakening: and like a flash, Miss X was reaching out to turn up the radio to its fullest volume so that the blast of pop music might drown the noise of the infant's crying while she hurriedly prepared the bottle. But before she could reach the knob, the sound which had awakened her came for a second time through the closed window, from the far end of the garden: words that she had never thought to hear again, in the voice of her own true daughter, not the little pretend daughter in the imitation crib:

"Mummy! Mummy! Mummy!"

CHAPTER 24

Nearly a year has passed, and it was summer again. Miranda had finished her O-levels, and though the results were not yet out, she felt pretty sure she'd done well. With the exams safely behind them, she and Sharon were busily preparing for the school trip to Greece; in the sunshine through her bedroom window, Miranda was sorting through the dresses, the tee shirts, the bikinis, and the slacks that were to be packed or not packed for the trip; a hard decision, for they were all becoming, and most of them new.

For that happy, mother-and-daughter shopping expedition which Mrs. Field had planned so disastrously a year ago, had, after all, taken place all these months later, exactly as she'd envisioned it, including the celebration Chinese lunch together after the main purchases had been successfully completed. It seemed almost impossible to believe, as they leaned towards each other, laughing and arguing over the elaborate menu, that that terrible period of misery, despair, and estrangement had been barely a year ago.

A hard year it had been, for both of them, the hardest in either of their lives; and yet, in another way, the most rewarding. Bitter lessons had been learned, but marvellous ones, too, which neither of them would ever forget.

Such as, that no single loss or disappointment can ruin a person's life forever, or even for very long: that no single blazing row, over no matter how important an issue, can destroy for any length of time a deep-rooted, loving relationship: that hatred and fury, however savage, have, in fact, a built-in life span that is intrinsically brief—if only because of the sheer effort involved in sustaining such feelings through the continual this, that, and the other of everyday life, ceaselessly draining away the victim's attention from the big, almighty grievance.

And, of course, in this case the big, almighty grievance had changed its nature almost beyond recognition during the days and weeks that followed the traumatic night when those baby clothes had come to light which Norah Field, in her role of "Miss X," had buried in her own garden. She'd hidden them there rather than in the dustbin for fear that the police might have organised a check on local dustbins for just such incriminating evidence; and, of course, she hadn't reckoned on someone like Iris noticing the disturbed soil, exploring it under cover of darkness, and jumping to the conclusion, on first glimpsing a baby garment, that the baby must be buried there, too. This conclusion of Iris's was not, actually, a wholly unreasonable one, given the data available to her. She could not have known, at that stage, that the baby in question was alive and well, less than a hundred yards away, comfortable and thriving nicely, thank you, under the care of its frantic, worn-out foster mother.

Perhaps not every three-week-old baby would have taken kindly to this shuffling back and forth between mothers: but Dawn was a tough little creature, both physically and mentally, and well able to fulfil the first and most important duty of every baby that is born onto this earth; the duty, that is of learning to get along with whatever sort of mother figure it finds itself landed with.

And meanwhile, other lessons were being learned. During the weeks of Norah Field's absence from home, recovering from what was called, for want of any better term, a "nervous breakdown," Miranda had to face the realisation which all children and young people have to face in the end: that those unassailable pillars of strength called parents have, after all, a breaking point; that the apparently helpless, put-upon child had it in his or her power to smash them into the ground; and easily. The first discovery of this power is terrifying, and takes some time to recover from.

The black-and-white zig-zag striped bikini would be best, Miranda decided, and slipped it into her suitcase, complete with plastic wrapping to preserve its pristine newness. The nearer this Greek trip approached, the more excited and happy she was feeling . . . and the more thoughtful, too.

Baby Caroline would have been five months old now. The miracle of pregnancy, the wonder and the glory of childbirth, would have been long over. By now, she, Miranda, would have been just one more Mum, plodding around with a pram, tied hand and foot day after day, week after week, until she was practically thirty. Right now, she'd be watching Sharon and her other friends setting off to Greece without her, not only leaving her out of the trip itself, but out of all the fun and excitement of the preparations. What would have been the point of including her in the laughter and the thrills of anticipation, when there was no way she could join them on the trip itself? By now, they'd have got used to leaving Miranda out of everything; what else could they do?

Would she *really* have been happy thus to have bartered away all the years of her youth in exchange for the joys of instant motherhood? Had it, indeed, been truly the joys of motherhood for which she'd yearned; or had it been, rather, the joys of fame, of showing off, of being one up on the other girls, of being a focus of wonder, awe, and admiration? Had it, in short, not been a *baby* that the abortion had deprived her of, but rather the biggest ego trip of all her young life . . . ?

Miranda had long ago forgiven her mother for the

awful trauma of the abortion; had come, painfully, to realise that the harsh and agonising decision really *had* hurt her mother very nearly as much as it had hurt herself, and had been prompted by the sincere belief that any other course would be the ruin of her daughter's future happiness. For a long time now Miranda had accepted, absolutely, that her mother's intentions had been of the best, and motivated solely by loving concern for Miranda herself; but only now, pressing down the lid of her shiny new suitcase to make it lock, did it suddenly cross her mind to wonder whether Mummy had not merely been well-intentioned, but might even, possibly, have been *right* . . . ?

She shrank away from the thought. It was too new; she wasn't ready for it, somehow. And there was much too much else to think about, anyway, this evening.

Delphi! They were going to see Delphi! In less than a week from now, she, Miranda Field, would be standing at the ancient shrine of Apollo, where, all those centuries ago, men, women, and maybe girls no older than herself had brought questions as intractable as her own, and had received answers from the god himself.

And yet, the answers hadn't always been right, as Greek history, with all its inter-city defeats and victories, amply proved. And if Apollo himself hadn't got all the answers, how could you expect Mummy to have them, either? Or Miranda herself, for that matter? What answers were there, anyway, that could be sure and certain? You just went forward, as best you could, in this direction or in that, and who could tell if the other, the different path would have proved better? Or proved worse . . . ?

"Miranda! Miranda, darling! Sharon's on the telephone, she wants to know if you've remembered about the guidebook to the Acropolis . . ."

How pleased and excited Mummy sounded, just as if *she* was the one to be going off on this marvellous trip, instead of being the one to be left at home coping with

Daddy's gloom about having lost the election! Well, naturally he'd lost it, without Mummy around during that crucial period of canvassing, he hadn't a hope. Everything he'd ever done had depended, always, on Mummy doing it for him.

Well, no, that wasn't *quite* true. And it had become even less true since those long weeks when Mummy had been away, and he'd *had* to cope with things. To telephone the plumber ***himself:*** to put his *own* arms round his daughter when he came upon her sobbing bitterly on the bottom step of the stairs. "Norah! Norah! Come quickly, that girl's crying again!" was no longer a complete and sufficient response to the situation.

Sometimes Miranda felt that she would remember till her dying day that first time when, through a blur of tears, she'd seen Daddy's tired, worried face staring at her in fear and bewilderment: and then how he'd slowly, uneasily taken off his gold-rimmed glasses in order to embrace her.

Having finished with the phone call from Sharon, complete with giggling and many a wild surmise about the days ahead, Miranda went back upstairs to complete her packing, and to check over what she might have forgotten.

Her address book, yes; there were lots of people she'd be wanting to send picture postcards to; she might even send one to the crowd at the Squat, just for the sake of keeping in touch, vaguely.

She'd imagined, when she first left the Squat in humiliation and headlong haste, that she'd never be able to face any of them again as long as she lived; but somehow, it hadn't worked out like that. First, Belinda had phoned; and then Tim had turned up with a load of her belongings, and had even stayed, quite friendly and without undue embarrassment, for a cup of coffee.

"Let us know how you get on, won't you, love?" he'd said, with a brotherly kiss, on parting; and after that it all began to seem not quite so absolutely frightful. She'd learned, in fact, one of the most important lessons in the whole of life; namely, that no one—no one at all—is one hundredth part as bothered about your humiliations as you are yourself. Within a week, whatever it is you've done, however shameful, no one—but *no one*—will be talking about it any more. They'll be talking about something else.

Some people take half a lifetime to learn this lesson; others never learn it at all; and so to have learned it by the age of fifteen is quite something.

Miranda paused, checking her address book. It was only barely worthwhile sending anything to the old address anyway, what with so many of them having left now: Alison back with her Mum and the Secretarial Course, and Iris having married a South American millionaire quite a bit older than herself, after what appeared like a whirlwind courtship.

"I'm damn well going to marry the very next man who asks me, I don't care *who* he is!" she'd been heard to announce during one particularly fraught evening just after Miranda's departure: and the fact that this randomly acquired gentleman should turn out to be a millionaire seemed to be just sheer luck—though of course with Iris you could never tell. No doubt she was in many ways just the right wife for a man trying to remain a millionaire during these devious and difficult financial days; and this, together with her decorative appearance, her efficiency, and her undisguised enthusiasm for providing him at top speed with an heir to the putative family millions, must have added up to a major attraction.

Anyway, marry him she did, and went off to South America. Tim, too, was gone, having taken up an appointment as a newly qualified Junior Registrar in a distant hospital. Even Christine had once more departed, having gone back to Keith—this time, taking her shoes with her: a gesture just about as near to "For better, for worse" as you could hope to find within the confines of her chosen life style.

So really, there was only Belinda left of the old crowd—except, of course, for—and here Miranda rummaged again through her address book. Yes, she really *must* send a postcard, if only to convey her congratulations.

Because while out on that shopping expedition with Mummy, they'd happened to pass a bookshop in the window of which was an eye-catching display of a new novel, flanked by ecstatic quotes from the reviews: "Gloriously understated mockery," "The send-up to end all send-ups!" were only some of the extravagant plaudits lavished by the critics upon the much talked of, best-selling satirical novel *Henry*.

